Selected Works of Edgar Allan Poe

Including Well-Known Poems and Stories
Written by Edgar Allan Poe
Edited by Valery J. Elias
Copyright©2023 by Valery J. Elias
All Rights Reserved
All works by Edgar Allan Poe are considered public domain.
Cover design by Valery Elias
Interior Art by Valery Elias

Tamerlane-first published in 1827
The Fall of the House of Usher-first published in
1839
The Murders in the Rue Morgue-first published in
1841
The Pit and the Pendulum-first published in 1842
The Tell-Tale Heart-first published in 1843
The Raven-first published in 1845

Edgar Allan Poe Biography

Edgar Allan Poe was born on January 1, 1909, in Boston to professional actors. However, before his third birthday, both his parents died. John and Frances Allan then raised Poe as a foster child in Richmond, Virginia. John was a successful tobacco exporter and sent Edgar to esteemed boarding schools before Poe went to the University of Virginia. Edgar was forced to leave school shortly thereafter when Allan refused to pay Edgar's gambling indebtedness.

Poe moved back to Boston, and during his brief stint there, published a book of poetry, "Tamerlane and Other Poems", using a pseudonym, " A Bostonian". Soon he joined the Army and then West Point, where he excelled but due to financial pressure, he had to leave and was court marshaled for dereliction of duty.

Poe later moved to Baltimore where he lived with relatives. He moved on from writing poetry to writing short stories, which turned out to be a pivotal moment. Poe is noted to be the first person to write a modern detective story- "The Murders in the Rue Morgue". His contributions to the horror genre are what set him apart from other mystery and detective story writers. His poem "The Raven" made him an overnight success and was published in 1845.

Poe died in 1849, his cause of death unknown, perhaps an apt end for the master of exquisite horror and mystery.

"All that we see or seem is but a dream within a dream."

Introduction

It was with morbid delight that I read aloud my report on The Premature Burial by Edgar Allan Poe to my freshman English class in high school almost 50 years ago. Watching not only the stunned faces of my peers, but my teacher as well, I was in my favorite creepy element, reveling in the discovery of Poe and his writing. From that day forward, I was hooked. Here, I've selected some of the best poems and stories that showcase Poe's mesmerizing ability to terrify. And so it begins... in no particular order.

The Pit and the Pendulum

Impia tortorum longos hic turba furores
Sanguinis innocui, non satiata, aluit.

Sospite nunc patria, fracto nunc funeris antro,
Mors ubi dira fuit vita salusque patent.
Translated this means: *Here the wicked mob, unappeased,*
long cherished a hatred of innocent blood. Now that the
fatherland is saved, and the cave of death demolished, where
grim death has been, life and health appear .
(Quatrain composed for the gates of a market to be erected
upon the site of the Jacobin Club House at Paris.)

I WAS sick – sick unto death with that long agony;
and when they at length unbound me, and I was
permitted to sit, I felt that my senses were leaving
me. The sentence – the dread sentence of death – was
the last of distinct accentuation which reached my
ears. After that, the sound of the inquisitorial voices
seemed merged in one dreamy indeterminate hum. It

conveyed to my soul the idea of revolution - perhaps from its association in fancy with the burr of a mill wheel. This only for a brief period; for presently I heard no more. Yet, for a while, I saw; but with how terrible an exaggeration! I saw the lips of the black-robed judges. They appeared to me white -- whiter than the sheet upon which I trace these words - and thin even to grotesqueness; thin with the intensity of their expression of firmness - of immoveable resolution - of stern contempt of human torture. I saw that the decrees of what to me was Fate, were still issuing from those lips. I saw them writhe with a deadly **locution** . I saw them fashion the syllables of my name; and I shuddered because no sound succeeded. I saw, too, for a few moments of delirious horror, the soft and nearly imperceptible waving of the sable draperies which enwrapped the walls of the apartment. And then my vision fell upon the seven tall candles upon the table. At first they wore the aspect of charity, and seemed white and slender angels who would save me; but then, all at once, there came a most deadly nausea over my spirit, and I felt every fibre in my frame thrill as if I had touched the wire of a galvanic battery, while the angel forms became meaningless spectres, with heads of flame, and I saw that from them there would be no help. And then there stole into my fancy, like a rich musical note, the thought of what sweet rest there must be in the grave. The thought came gently and stealthily, and it seemed long before it attained full appreciation; but just as my spirit came at length properly to feel and entertain it, the figures of the judges vanished, as if magically, from before me; the tall candles sank into nothingness; their flames went out utterly; the blackness of darkness supervened; all sensations appeared swallowed up in a mad rushing descent as of the soul into Hades. Then silence, and stillness, night were the universe.

I had swooned; but still will not say that all of consciousness was lost. What of it there remained I will not attempt to define, or even to describe; yet all was not lost. In the deepest slumber - no! In delirium - no! In a swoon - no! In death -- no! even in the grave all is not lost. Else there is no immortality for man. Arousing from the most profound of slumbers, we break the **gossamer** web of *some* dream. Yet in a second afterward, (so frail may that web have been) we remember not that we have dreamed. In the return to life from the swoon there are two stages; first, that of the sense of mental or spiritual; secondly, that of the sense of physical, existence. It seems probable that if, upon reaching the second stage, we could recall the impressions of the first, we should find these impressions eloquent in memories of the gulf beyond. And that gulf is -- what? How at least shall we distinguish its shadows from those of the tomb? But if the impressions of what I have termed the first stage, are not, at will, recalled, yet, after long interval, do they not come unbidden, while we marvel whence they come? He who has never swooned, is not he who finds strange palaces and wildly familiar faces in coals that glow; is not he who beholds floating in mid-air the sad visions that the many may not view; is not he who ponders over the perfume of some novel flower -- is not he whose brain grows bewildered with the meaning of some musical cadence which has never before arrested his attention.

Amid frequent and thoughtful endeavors to remember; amid earnest struggles to regather some token of the state of seeming nothingness into which my soul had lapsed, there have been moments when I have dreamed of success; there have been brief, very brief periods when I have conjured up remembrances which the lucid reason of a later epoch assures me could have had reference only to that condition of seeming unconsciousness. These shadows of memory tell, indistinctly, of tall figures that lifted and bore me in silence down - down - still down -till a hideous dizziness oppressed me at the mere idea of the interminableness of the descent. They tell also of a vague horror at my heart, on account of that heart's unnatural stillness. Then comes a sense of sudden motionlessness throughout all things; as if those who bore me (a ghastly train!) had outrun, in their descent, the limits of the limitless, and paused from the wearisomeness of their toil. After this I call to mind flatness and dampness; and then all is madness -- the madness of a memory which busies itself among forbidden things.

Very suddenly there came back to my soul motion and sound - the tumultuous motion of the heart, and, in my ears, the sound of its beating. Then a pause in which all is blank. Then again sound, and motion, and touch - a tingling sensation pervading my frame. Then the mere consciousness of existence, without thought -a condition which lasted long. Then, very suddenly, thought, and shuddering terror, and earnest endeavor to comprehend my true state. Then a strong desire to lapse into insensibility. Then a rushing revival of soul and a successful effort to move. And now a full memory of the trial, of the judges, of the sable draperies, of the sentence, of the sickness, of the swoon. Then entire forgetfulness of all that followed; of all that a later day and much earnestness of endeavor have enabled me vaguely to recall.

So far, I had not opened my eyes. I felt that I lay upon my back, unbound. I reached out my hand, and it fell heavily upon something damp and hard. There I suffered it to remain for many minutes, while I strove to imagine where and what I could be. I longed, yet dared not to employ my vision. I dreaded the first glance at objects around me. It was not that I feared to look upon things horrible, but that I grew aghast lest there should be nothing to see. At length, with a wild desperation at heart, I quickly unclosed my eyes. My worst thoughts, then, were confirmed. The blackness of eternal night encompassed me. I struggled for breath. The intensity of the darkness seemed to oppress and stifle me. The atmosphere was intolerably close. I still lay quietly, and made effort to exercise my reason. I brought to mind the inquisitorial proceedings, and attempted from that point to deduce my real condition. The sentence had passed; and it appeared to me that a very long interval of time had since elapsed. Yet not for a moment did I suppose myself actually dead. Such a supposition, notwithstanding what we read in fiction, is altogether inconsistent with real existence; -- but where and in what state was I? The condemned to death, I knew, perished usually at the autos-da-fe, and one of these had been held on the very night of the day of my trial. Had I been remanded to my dungeon, to await the next sacrifice, which would not take place for many months? This I at once saw could not be. Victims had been in immediate demand. Moreover, my dungeon, as well as all the condemned cells at Toledo , had stone floors, and light was not altogether excluded. A fearful idea now suddenly drove the blood in torrents upon my heart, and for a brief period, I once more relapsed into insensibility. Upon recovering, I at once started to my feet, trembling convulsively in every fibre. I thrust my arms wildly above and around me in all directions. I felt nothing; yet dreaded to move a step, lest I should be impeded by the walls of a tomb. Perspiration burst from every pore, and stood in cold big beads upon my forehead. The agony of suspense grew at length intolerable, and I cautiously moved forward, with my arms extended, and my eyes straining from their sockets, in the hope of catching some faint ray of light. I proceeded for many paces; but still all was blackness and vacancy. I breathed more freely. It seemed evident that mine was not, at least, the most hideous of fates.

And now, as I still continued to step cautiously onward, there came thronging upon my recollection a thousand vague rumors of the horrors of **Toledo** . Of the dungeons there had been strange things narrated -- fables I had always deemed them -- but yet strange, and too ghastly to repeat, save in a whisper. Was I left to perish of starvation in this subterranean world of darkness; or what fate, perhaps even more fearful, awaited me? That the result would be death, and a death of more than customary bitterness, I knew too well the character of my judges to doubt. The mode and the hour were all that occupied or distracted me.

My outstretched hands at length encountered some solid obstruction. It was a wall, seemingly of stone masonry - very smooth, slimy, and cold. I followed it up; stepping with all the careful distrust with which certain antique narratives had inspired me. This process, however, afforded me no means of ascertaining the dimensions of my dungeon; as I might make its circuit, and return to the point whence I set out, without being aware of the fact; so perfectly uniform seemed the wall. I therefore sought the knife which had been in my pocket, when led into the inquisitorial chamber; but it was gone; my clothes had been exchanged for a wrapper of coarse serge. I had thought of forcing the blade in some minute crevice of the masonry, so as to identify my point of departure. The difficulty, nevertheless, was but trivial; although, in the disorder of my fancy, it seemed at first insuperable. I tore a part of the hem from the robe and placed the

fragment at full length, and at right angles to the
wall. In groping my way around the prison, I could
not fail to encounter this rag upon completing the
circuit. So, at least I thought: but I had not counted
upon the extent of the dungeon, or upon my own
weakness. The ground was moist and slippery. I
staggered onward for some time, when I stumbled
and fell. My excessive fatigue induced me to remain
prostrate; and sleep soon overtook me as I lay.
Upon awaking, and stretching forth an arm, I found
beside me a loaf and a pitcher with water. I was too
much exhausted to reflect upon this circumstance,
but ate and drank with avidity. Shortly afterward, I
resumed my tour around the prison, and with much
toil came at last upon the fragment of the serge. Up
to the period when I fell I had counted fifty-two
paces, and upon resuming my walk, I had counted
forty-eight more; -- when I arrived at the rag. There
were in all, then, a hundred paces; and, admitting
two paces to the yard, I presumed the dungeon to be
fifty yards in circuit. I had met, however, with many
angles in the wall, and thus I could form no guess at
the shape of the vault; for vault I could not help
supposing it to be.
I had little object – certainly no hope these
researches; but a vague curiosity prompted me to
continue them. Quitting the wall, I resolved to cross
the area of the enclosure. At first I proceeded with
extreme caution, for the floor, although seemingly of
solid material, was treacherous with slime. At
length, however, I took courage, and did not hesitate
to step firmly; endeavoring to cross in as direct a

line as possible. I had advanced some ten or twelve paces in this manner, when the remnant of the torn hem of my robe became entangled between my legs. I stepped on it, and fell violently on my face.
In the confusion attending my fall, I did not immediately apprehend a somewhat startling circumstance, which yet, in a few seconds afterward, and while I still lay prostrate, arrested my attention. It was this -- my chin rested upon the floor of the prison, but my lips and the upper portion of my head, although seemingly at a less elevation than the chin, touched nothing. At the same time my forehead seemed bathed in a clammy vapor, and the peculiar smell of decayed fungus arose to my nostrils. I put forward my arm, and shuddered to find that I had fallen at the very brink of a circular pit, whose extent, of course, I had no means of ascertaining at the moment. Groping about the masonry just below the margin, I succeeded in dislodging a small fragment, and let it fall into the abyss. For many seconds I hearkened to its reverberations as it dashed against the sides of the chasm in its descent; at length there was a **sullen** plunge into water, succeeded by loud echoes. At the same moment there came a sound resembling the quick opening, and as rapid closing of a door overhead, while a faint gleam of light flashed suddenly through the gloom, and as suddenly faded away.
I saw clearly the doom which had been prepared for me, and congratulated myself upon the timely accident by which I had escaped. Another step before

my fall, and the world had seen me no more. And the death just avoided, was of that very character which I had regarded as fabulous and frivolous in the tales respecting the Inquisition . To the victims of its tyranny, there was the choice of death with its direst physical agonies, or death with its most hideous moral horrors. I had been reserved for the latter. By long suffering my nerves had been unstrung, until I trembled at the sound of my own voice, and had become in every respect a fitting subject for the species of torture which awaited me.

Shaking in every limb, I groped my way back to the wall; resolving there to perish rather than risk the terrors of the wells, of which my imagination now pictured many in various positions about the dungeon. In other conditions of mind I might have had courage to end my misery at once by a plunge into one of these abysses; but now I was the veriest of cowards. Neither could I forget what I had read of these pits -- that the sudden extinction of life formed no part of their most horrible plan. Agitation of spirit kept me awake for many long hours; but at length I again slumbered. Upon arousing, I found by my side, as before, a loaf and a pitcher of water. A burning thirst consumed me, and I emptied the vessel at a **draught** . It must have been drugged; for scarcely had I drunk, before I became irresistibly drowsy. A deep sleep fell upon me -- a sleep like that of death. How long it lasted of course, I know not; but when, once again, I unclosed my eyes, the objects around me were visible. By a wild sulphurous lustre, the origin of which I could not at first determine, I was enabled to see the extent and aspect of the prison.

In its size I had been greatly mistaken. The whole circuit of its walls did not exceed twenty-five yards. For some minutes this fact occasioned me a world of vain trouble; vain indeed! for what could be of less importance, under the terrible circumstances which environed me, then the mere dimensions of my dungeon? But my soul took a wild interest in trifles, and I busied myself in endeavors to account for the error I had committed in my measurement. The truth at length flashed upon me. In my first attempt at exploration I had counted fifty-two paces, up to the period when I fell; I must then have been within a pace or two of the fragment of serge; in fact, I had nearly performed the circuit of the vault. I then slept, and upon awaking, I must have returned upon my steps -thus supposing the circuit nearly double what it actually was. My confusion of mind prevented me from observing that I began my tour with the wall to the left, and ended it with the wall to the right.

I had been deceived, too, in respect to the shape of the enclosure. In feeling my way I had found many angles, and thus deduced an idea of great irregularity; so potent is the effect of total darkness upon one arousing from lethargy or sleep! The angles were simply those of a few slight depressions, or niches, at odd intervals. The general shape of the prison was square. What I had taken for masonry seemed now to be iron, or some other metal, in huge plates, whose sutures or joints occasioned the depression. The entire surface of this metallic enclosure was rudely daubed in all the hideous and repulsive devices to which the charnel superstition of the monks has given rise. The figures of fiends in aspects of menace, with skeleton forms, and other more really fearful images, overspread and disfigured the walls. I observed that the outlines of these monstrosities were sufficiently distinct, but that the colors seemed faded and blurred, as if from the effects of a damp atmosphere. I now noticed the floor, too, which was of stone. In the centre yawned the circular pit from whose jaws I had escaped; but it was the only one in the dungeon.

All this I saw indistinctly and by much effort: for my personal condition had been greatly changed during slumber. I now lay upon my back, and at full length, on a species of low framework of wood. To this I was securely bound by a long strap resembling a surcingle . It passed in many convolutions about my limbs and body, leaving at liberty only my head, and my left arm to such extent that I could, by dint of much exertion, supply myself with food from an earthen dish which lay by my side on the floor. I saw, to my horror, that the pitcher had been removed. I say to my horror; for I was consumed with intolerable thirst. This thirst it appeared to be the design of my persecutors to stimulate: for the food in the dish was meat pungently seasoned. Looking upward, I surveyed the ceiling of my prison. It was some thirty or forty feet overhead, and constructed much as the side walls. In one of its panels a very singular figure riveted my whole attention. It was the painted figure of Time as he is commonly represented, save that, in lieu of a   scythe , he held what, at a casual glance, I supposed to be the pictured image of a huge pendulum such as we see on antique clocks. There was something, however, in the appearance of this machine which caused me to regard it more attentively. While I gazed directly upward at it (for its position was immediately over my own) I fancied that I saw it in motion. In an instant afterward the fancy was confirmed. Its sweep was brief, and of course slow. I watched it for some minutes, somewhat in fear, but more in wonder. Wearied at length with observing its dull movement, I turned my eyes upon the other objects in the cell.

A slight noise attracted my notice, and, looking to the floor, I saw several enormous rats traversing it. They had issued from the well, which lay just within view to my right. Even then, while I gazed, they came up in troops, hurriedly, with ravenous eyes, allured by the scent of the meat. From this it required much effort and attention to scare them away.

It might have been half an hour, perhaps even an hour, (for I could take but imperfect note of time) before I again cast my eyes upward. What I then saw confounded and amazed me. The sweep of the pendulum had increased in extent by nearly a yard. As a natural consequence, its velocity was also much greater. But what mainly disturbed me was the idea that had perceptibly descended. I now observed - with what horror it is needless to say -- that its nether extremity was formed of a crescent of glittering steel, about a foot in length from horn to horn; the horns upward, and the under edge evidently as keen as that of a razor. Like a razor also, it seemed massy and heavy, tapering from the edge into a solid and broad structure above. It was appended to a weighty rod of brass, and the whole hissed as it swung through the air.

I could no longer doubt the doom prepared for me by monkish ingenuity in torture. My cognizance of *the pit* had become known to the inquisitorial agents – the pit whose horrors had been destined for so bold a recusant as myself – the pit, typical of hell, and regarded by rumor as the Ultima Thule of all their punishments. The plunge into this pit I had avoided by the merest of accidents, I knew that surprise, or entrapment into torment, formed an important portion of all the grotesquerie of these dungeon deaths. Having failed to fall, it was no part of the demon plan to hurl me into the abyss; and thus (there being no alternative) a different and a milder destruction awaited me. Milder! I half smiled in my agony as I thought of such application of such a term.

What boots it to tell of the long, long hours of horror more than mortal, during which I counted the rushing vibrations of the steel! Inch by inch – line by line – with a descent only appreciable at intervals that seemed ages – down and still down it came! Days passed – it might have been that many days passed – ere it swept so closely over me as to fan me with its acrid breath. The odor of the sharp steel

forced itself into my nostrils. I prayed - I wearied heaven with my prayer for its more speedy descent. I grew frantically mad, and struggled to force myself upward against the sweep of the fearful scimitar . And then I fell suddenly calm, and lay smiling at the glittering death, as a child at some rare bauble . There was another interval of utter insensibility; it was brief; for, upon again lapsing into life there had been no perceptible descent in the pendulum. But it might have been long; for I knew there were demons who took note of my swoon, and who could have arrested the vibration at pleasure. Upon my recovery, too, I felt very - oh, inexpressibly sick and weak, as if through long **inanition** . Even amid the agonies of that period, the human nature craved food. With painful effort I outstretched my left arm as far as my bonds permitted, and took possession of the small remnant which had been spared me by the rats. As I put a portion of it within my lips, there rushed to my mind a half formed thought of joy - of hope. Yet what business had I with hope? It was, as I say, a half formed thought - man has many such which are never completed. I felt that it was of joy - of hope; but felt also that it had perished in its formation. In vain I struggled to perfect - to regain it. Long suffering had nearly annihilated all my ordinary powers of mind. I was an imbecile -- an idiot.
The vibration of the pendulum was at right angles to my length. I saw that the crescent was designed to cross the region of the heart. It would fray the serge of my robe - it would return and repeat its operations - again - and again. Notwithstanding

terrifically wide sweep (some thirty feet or more)
and the hissing vigor of its descent, sufficient to
sunder these very walls of iron, still the fraying of
my robe would be all that, for several minutes, it
would accomplish. And at this thought I paused. I
dared not go farther than this reflection. I dwelt
upon it with a pertinacity of attention -as if, in so
dwelling, I could arrest here the descent of the steel.
I forced myself to ponder upon the sound of the
crescent as it should pass across the garment - upon
the peculiar thrilling sensation which the friction of
cloth produces on the nerves. I pondered upon all
this frivolity until my teeth were on edge.

Down - steadily down it crept. I took a frenzied
pleasure in contrasting its downward with its lateral
velocity. To the right - to the left -far and wide -
with the shriek of a damned spirit; to my heart with
the stealthy pace of the tiger! I alternately laughed
and howled as one or the other idea grew
predominant.

Down - certainly, relentlessly down! It vibrated
within three inches of my bosom! I struggled
violently, furiously, to free my left arm. This was
free only from the elbow to the hand. I could reach
the latter, from the platter beside me, to my mouth,
with great effort, but no farther. Could I have broken
the fastenings above the elbow, I would have seized
and attempted to arrest the pendulum. I might as
well have attempted to arrest an avalanche!

Down - still unceasingly - still inevitably down! I
gasped and struggled at each vibration. I shrunk
convulsively at its every sweep. My eyes followed its

outward or upward whirls with the eagerness of the most unmeaning despair; they closed themselves spasmodically at the descent, although death would have been a relief, oh! how unspeakable! Still I quivered in every nerve to think how slight a sinking of the machinery would precipitate that keen, glistening axe upon my bosom. It was hope that prompted the nerve to quiver - the frame to shrink. It was hope - the hope that triumphs on the rack - that whispers to the death-condemned even in the dungeons of the Inquisition .

I saw that some ten or twelve vibrations would bring the steel in actual contact with my robe, and with this observation there suddenly came over my spirit all the keen, collected calmness of despair. For the first time during many hours - or perhaps days -I thought. It now occurred to me that the bandage, or surcingle , which enveloped me, was unique. I was tied by no separate cord. The first stroke of the razorlike crescent athwart any portion of the band, would so detach it that it might be unwound from my person by means of my left hand. But how fearful, in that case, the proximity of the steel! The result of the slightest struggle how deadly! Was it likely, moreover, that the minions of the torturer had not foreseen and provided for this possibility! Was it probable that the bandage crossed my bosom in the track of the pendulum? Dreading to find my faint, and, as it seemed, in last hope frustrated, I so far elevated my head as to obtain a distinct view of my breast. The surcingle enveloped my limbs and body close in all directions –save in the path of the destroying crescent.

Scarcely had I dropped my head back into its original position, when there flashed upon my mind what I cannot better describe than as the unformed half of that idea of deliverance to which I have previously alluded, and of which a **moiety** only floated indeterminately through my brain when I raised food to my burning lips. The whole thought was now present – feeble, scarcely sane, scarcely definite, – but still entire. I proceeded at once, with the nervous energy of despair, to attempt its execution.

For many hours the immediate vicinity of the low framework upon which I lay, had been literally swarming with rats. They were wild, bold, ravenous; their red eyes glaring upon me as if they waited but for motionlessness on my part to make me their prey. "To what food," I thought, "have they been accustomed in the well?"

They had devoured, in spite of all my efforts to prevent them, all but a small remnant of the contents of the dish. I had fallen into an habitual see–saw, or wave of the hand about the platter: and, at length, the unconscious uniformity of the movement deprived it of effect. In their voracity the vermin frequently fastened their sharp fangs in my fingers. With the particles of the oily and spicy viand which now remained, I thoroughly rubbed the bandage wherever I could reach it; then, raising my hand from the floor, I lay breathlessly still.

At first the ravenous animals were startled and terrified at the change – at the cessation of

movement. They shrank alarmedly back; many sought the well. But this was only for a moment. I had not counted in vain upon their voracity. Observing that I remained without motion, one or two of the boldest leaped upon the frame-work, and smelt at the surcingle . This seemed the signal for a general rush. Forth from the well they hurried in fresh troops. They clung to the wood – they overran it, and leaped in hundreds upon my person. The measured movement of the pendulum disturbed them not at all. Avoiding its strokes they busied themselves with the anointed bandage. They pressed – they swarmed upon me in ever accumulating heaps. They writhed upon my throat; their cold lips sought my own; I was half stifled by their thronging pressure; disgust, for which the world has no name, swelled my bosom, and chilled, with a heavy clamminess, my heart. Yet one minute, and I felt that the struggle would be over. Plainly I perceived the loosening of the bandage. I knew that in more than one place it must be already severed. With a more than human resolution I lay still.
Nor had I erred in my calculations – nor had I endured in vain. I at length felt that I was free. The surcingle hung in ribands from my body. But the stroke of the pendulum already pressed upon my bosom. It had divided the serge of the robe. It had cut through the linen beneath. Twice again it swung, and a sharp sense of pain shot through every nerve. But the moment of escape had arrived. At a wave of my hand my deliverers hurried tumultuously away. With a steady movement –cautious, sidelong,

shrinking, and slow - I slid from the embrace of the bandage and beyond the reach of the scimitar . For the moment, at least, I was free.

Free! - and in the grasp of the Inquisition ! I had scarcely stepped from my wooden bed of horror upon the stone floor of the prison, when the motion of the hellish machine ceased and I beheld it drawn up, by some invisible force, through the ceiling. This was a lesson which I took desperately to heart. My every motion was undoubtedly watched. Free! -I had but escaped death in one form of agony, to be delivered unto worse than death in some other. With that thought I rolled my eyes nervously around on the barriers of iron that hemmed me in. Something unusual -some change which, at first, I could not appreciate distinctly - it was obvious, had taken place in the apartment. For many minutes of a dreamy and trembling abstraction, I busied myself in vain, unconnected conjecture. During this period, I became aware, for the first time, of the origin of the sulphurous light which illumined the cell. It proceeded from a fissure, about half an inch in width, extending entirely around the prison at the base of the walls, which thus appeared, and were, completely separated from the floor. I endeavored, but of course in vain, to look through the aperture . As I arose from the attempt, the mystery of the alteration in the chamber broke at once upon my understanding. I have observed that, although the outlines of the figures upon the walls were sufficiently distinct, yet the colors seemed blurred and indefinite. These colors had now assumed, and were momentarily assuming, a startling and most intense brilliancy, that gave to the spectral and fiendish portraitures an aspect that might have thrilled even firmer nerves than my own. Demon eyes, of a wild and ghastly vivacity, glared upon me in a thousand directions, where none had been visible before, and gleamed with the lurid lustre of a fire that I could not force my imagination to regard as unreal.

Unreal! – Even while I breathed there came to my nostrils the breath of the vapour of heated iron! A suffocating odour pervaded the prison! A deeper glow settled each moment in the eyes that glared at my agonies! A richer tint of crimson diffused itself over the pictured horrors of blood. I panted! I gasped for breath! There could be no doubt of the design of my tormentors - oh! most unrelenting! oh! most demoniac of men! I shrank from the glowing metal to the centre of the cell. Amid the thought of the fiery destruction that impended, the idea of the coolness of the well came over my soul like balm. I rushed to its deadly brink. I threw my straining vision below. The glare from the enkindled roof illumined its inmost recesses. Yet, for a wild moment, did my spirit refuse to comprehend the meaning of what I saw. At length it forced - it wrestled its way into my soul - it burned itself in upon my shuddering reason. - Oh! for a voice to speak! - oh! horror! - oh! any horror but this! With a shriek, I rushed from the margin, and buried my face in my hands - weeping bitterly.

The heat rapidly increased, and once again I looked up, shuddering as with a fit of the ague. There had been a second change in the cell - and now the change was obviously in the form. As before, it was in vain that I, at first, endeavoured to appreciate or understand what was taking place. But not long was I left in doubt. The Inquisitorial vengeance had been hurried by my two-fold escape, and there was to be no more dallying with the King of Terrors. The room had been square. I saw that two of its iron angles were now acute - two, consequently, obtuse . The fearful difference quickly increased with a low rumbling or moaning sound. In an instant the apartment had shifted its form into that of a lozenge. But the alteration stopped not here-I neither hoped nor desired it to stop. I could have clasped the red walls to my bosom as a garment of eternal peace. "Death," I said, "any death but that of the pit!" Fool! might I have not known that into the pit it was the object of the burning iron to urge me? Could I resist its glow? or, if even that, could I withstand its pressure And now, flatter and flatter grew the lozenge, with a rapidity that left me no time for contemplation. Its centre, and of course, its greatest width, came just over the yawning gulf. I shrank back - but the closing walls pressed me resistlessly onward. At length for my seared and writhing body there was no longer an inch of foothold on the firm floor of the prison. I struggled no more, but the agony of my soul found vent in one loud, long, and final scream of despair. I felt that I tottered upon the brink - I averted my eyes --

There was a discordant hum of human voices! There was a loud blast as of many trumpets! There was a harsh grating as of a thousand thunders! The fiery walls rushed back! An outstretched arm caught my own as I fell, fainting, into the abyss. It was that of General Lasalle . The French army had entered Toledo . The Inquisition was in the hands of its enemies.

The Tell-Tale Heart

TRUE!—nervous—very, very dreadfully nervous I had been and am; but why will you say that I am mad? The disease had sharpened my senses—not destroyed—not dulled them. Above all was the sense of hearing acute. I heard all things in the heaven and in the earth. I heard many things in hell. How, then, am I mad? Hearken! and observe how healthily— how calmly I can tell you the whole story. It is impossible to say how first the idea entered my brain; but once conceived, it haunted me day and night. Object there was none. Passion there was none. I loved the old man. He had never wronged me. He had never given me insult. For his gold I had no desire. I think it was his eye! yes, it was this! One of his eyes resembled that of a vulture—a pale blue eye, with a film over it. Whenever it fell upon me, my blood ran cold; and so by degrees—very gradually—I made up my mind to take the life of the old man, and thus rid myself of the eye for ever. Now this is the point. You fancy me mad. Madmen know nothing. But you should have seen me. You should have seen how wisely I proceeded—with what caution— with what foresight—with what dissimulation I went to work! I was never kinder to the old man than during the whole week before I killed him. And every night, about midnight, I turned the latch of his door and opened it—oh, so gently! And then, when I had made an opening sufficient for my head, I put in a dark lantern, all closed, closed, so that no light shone out, and then I thrust in my head. Oh, you would have laughed to

see how cunningly I thrust it in! I moved it slowly—
very, very slowly, so that I might not disturb the old
man's sleep. It took me an hour to place my whole
head within the opening so far that I could see him
as he lay upon 4 THE TELL-TALE HEART his bed.
Ha!—would a madman have been so wise as this?
And then, when my head was well in the room, I
undid the lantern cautiously—oh, so cautiously—
cautiously (for the hinges creaked)—I undid it just
so much that a single thin ray fell upon the vulture
eye. And this I did for seven long nights—every
night just at midnight—but I found the eye always
closed, and so it was impossible to do the work; for
it was not the old man who vexed me, but his Evil
Eye. And every morning, when the day broke, I went
boldly into the chamber, and spoke courageously to
him, calling him by name in a hearty tone, and
inquiring how he had passed the night. So you see he
would have been a very profound old man, indeed, to
suspect that every night, just at twelve, I looked in
upon him while he slept. Upon the eighth night I
was more than usually cautious in opening the door.
A watch's minute hand moves more quickly than did
mine. Never before that night had I felt the extent of
my own powers—of my sagacity. I could scarcely
contain my feelings of triumph. To think that there I
was, opening the door, little by little, and he not
even to dream of my secret deeds or thoughts. I
fairly chuckled at the idea; and perhaps he heard me;
for he moved on the bed suddenly, as if startled.
Now you may think that I drew back—but no. His
room was as black as pitch with the thick darkness
(for the shutters were close fastened, through fear of
robbers), and so I knew that he could not see the

opening of the door, and I kept pushing it on steadily, steadily. I had my head in, and was about to open the lantern, when my thumb slipped upon the tin fastening, and the old man sprang up in the bed, crying out—"Who's there?" I kept quite still and said nothing. For a whole hour I did not move a muscle, and in the meantime I did not hear him lie down. He was still sitting up in the bed listening;—EDGAR ALLAN POE 5 just as I have done, night after night, hearkening to the death watches in the wall. Presently I heard a slight groan, and I knew it was the groan of mortal terror. It was not a groan of pain or of grief—oh, no!—it was the low stifled sound that arises from the bottom of the soul when overcharged with awe. I knew the sound well. Many a night, just at midnight, when all the world slept, it has welled up from my own bosom, deepening, with its dreadful echo, the terrors that distracted me. I say I knew it well. I knew what the old man felt, and pitied him, although I chuckled at heart. I knew that he had been lying awake ever since the first slight noise, when he had turned in the bed. His fears had been ever since growing upon him. He had been trying to fancy them causeless, but could not. He had been saying to himself—"It is nothing but the wind in the chimney—it is only a mouse crossing the floor," or "it is merely a cricket which has made a single chirp." Yes, he has been trying to comfort himself with these suppositions; but he had found all in vain. All in vain; because Death, in approaching him, had stalked with his black shadow before him, and enveloped the victim. And it was the mournful influence of the unperceived shadow that caused him to feel—although he neither saw nor heard—to feel the presence of my head within the room. When I had waited a long time, very patiently, without hearing him lie down, I resolved to open a little—a very, very little crevice in the lantern. So I opened it—you cannot imagine how stealthily, stealthily—until, at length, a single dim ray, like the thread of the spider, shot from out the crevice and full upon the vulture eye. It was open—wide, wide open—and I grew furious as I gazed upon it. I saw it with perfect distinctness—all a dull blue, with a hideous veil over it that chilled the very marrow in my bones; but I could see nothing else of the old man's 6 THE TELL-TALE HEART face or person: for I had directed the ray as if by instinct, precisely upon the damned spot. And now have I not told you that what you mistake for madness is but over-acuteness of the senses?—now, I say, there came to my ears a low, dull, quick sound, such as a watch makes when enveloped in cotton. I knew that sound well too. It was the beating of the old man's heart. It increased my fury, as the beating of a drum stimulates the soldier into courage. But even yet I refrained and kept still. I scarcely breathed. I held the lantern motionless. I tried how steadily I could maintain the ray upon the eye. Meantime the hellish tattoo of the heart increased. It grew quicker and quicker, and louder and louder every instant. The old man's terror must have been extreme! It grew louder, I say, louder every moment!—do you mark me well? I have told you that I am nervous: so I am. And now at the dead hour of the night, amid the dreadful silence of that old house, so strange a noise as this excited me to uncontrollable terror. Yet, for some minutes longer I refrained and stood still. But the beating grew louder, louder! I thought the heart must burst. And now a new anxiety seized me—the sound would be heard by a neighbor! The old man's hour had come! With a loud yell, I threw open the lantern and leaped into the room. He shrieked once—once only. In an instant I dragged him to the floor, and pulled the heavy bed over him. I then smiled gaily, to find the deed so far done. But, for many minutes, the heart beat on with a muffled sound. This, however, did not vex me; it would not be heard through the wall. At length it ceased. The old man was dead. I removed the bed and examined the corpse. Yes, he was stone, stone dead. I placed my hand upon the heart and held it there many minutes. There was no pulsation. He was stone dead. His eye would trouble me no more. If still you think me mad, you will think so no longer when I describe the wise precautions I took for the concealment of the body. The night waned, and I worked hastily, but in silence. First of all I dismembered the corpse. I cut off the head and the arms and the legs. I then took up three planks from the flooring of the chamber, and deposited all between the scantlings. I then replaced the boards so cleverly, so cunningly, that no human eye—not even his—could have detected any thing wrong. There was nothing to wash out—no stain of any kind—no blood-spot whatever. I had been too wary for that. A tub had caught all—ha! ha! When I had made an end of these labors, it was four o'clock—still dark as midnight. As the bell sounded the hour, there came a knocking at the street door. I went down to open it with a light heart,—for what had I now to fear? There entered three men, who introduced themselves, with perfect suavity, as officers of the police. A shriek had been heard by a neighbor during the night; suspicion of foul play had been aroused; information had been lodged at the police office, and they (the officers) had been deputed to search the premises. I smiled,— for what had I to fear? I bade the gentlemen welcome. The shriek, I said, was my own in a dream. The old man, I mentioned, was absent in the country. I took my visitors all over the house. I bade them search—search well. I led them, at length, to his chamber. I showed them his treasures, secure, undisturbed. In the enthusiasm of my confidence, I brought chairs into the room, and desired them here to rest from their fatigues, while I myself, in the wild audacity of my perfect triumph, placed my own seat upon the very spot beneath which reposed the corpse of the victim. The officers were satisfied. My manner had convinced them. I was singularly at ease. They sat, and while I 8 THE TELL-TALE HEART answered cheerily, they chatted of familiar things. But, ere long, I felt myself getting pale and wished them gone. My head ached, and I fancied a ringing in my ears: but still they sat and still chatted. The ringing became more distinct:—it continued and became more distinct: I talked more freely to get rid of the feeling: but it continued and gained definitiveness—until, at length, I found that the noise was not within my ears. No doubt I now grew very pale;—but I talked more fluently, and with a heightened voice. Yet the sound increased— and what could I do? It was a low, dull, quick sound—much such a sound as a watch makes when enveloped in cotton. I gasped for breath—and yet the officers heard it not. I talked more quickly—

more vehemently; but the noise steadily increased. I arose and argued about trifles, in a high key and with violent gesticulations, but the noise steadily increased. Why would they not be gone? I paced the floor to and fro with heavy strides, as if excited to fury by the observation of the men—but the noise steadily increased. Oh God! what could I do? I foamed—I raved—I swore! I swung the chair upon which I had been sitting, and grated it upon the boards, but the noise arose over all and continually increased. It grew louder—louder—louder! And still the men chatted pleasantly, and smiled. Was it possible they heard not? Almighty God!—no, no! They heard!—they suspected!—they knew!—they were making a mockery of my horror!—this I thought, and this I think. But any thing was better than this agony! Any thing was more tolerable than this derision! I could bear those hypocritical smiles no longer! I felt that I must scream or die!—and now—again!— hark! louder! louder! louder! louder!— "Villains!" I shrieked, "dissemble no more! I admit the deed!—tear up the planks!—here, here!—it is the beating of his hideous heart."

The Raven

Once upon a midnight dreary, while I pondered, weak and weary,
Over many a quaint and curious volume of forgotten lore—
While I nodded, nearly napping, suddenly there came a tapping,
As of some one gently rapping, rapping at my chamber door—
"'Tis some visitor," I muttered, "tapping at my chamber door—
          Only this and nothing more."

Ah, distinctly I remember it was in the bleak December;
And each separate dying ember wrought its ghost upon the floor.
Eagerly I wished the morrow;—vainly I had sought to borrow
From my books surcease of sorrow—sorrow for the lost Lenore—
For the rare and radiant maiden whom the angels name Lenore—
      Nameless *here* for evermore.
And the silken, sad, uncertain rustling of each purple curtain
Thrilled me—filled me with fantastic terrors never felt before;
So that now, to still the beating of my heart, I stood repeating,
"'Tis some visitor entreating entrance at my chamber door—
Some late visitor entreating entrance at my chamber door;—
      This it is and nothing more."
Presently my soul grew stronger; hesitating then no longer,
"Sir," said I, "or Madam, truly your forgiveness I implore;
But the fact is I was napping, and so gently you came rapping,
And so faintly you came tapping, tapping at my chamber door,
That I scarce was sure I heard you"—here I opened wide the door;—
      Darkness there and nothing more.
Deep into that darkness peering, long I stood there wondering, fearing,

Doubting, dreaming dreams no mortal ever dared to
dream before;
But the silence was unbroken, and the stillness gave
no token,
And the only word there spoken was the whispered
word, "Lenore?"
This I whispered, and an echo murmured back the
word, "Lenore!"—
   Merely this and nothing more.
Back into the chamber turning, all my soul within me
burning,
Soon again I heard a tapping somewhat louder than
before.
"Surely," said I, "surely that is something at my
window lattice;
Let me see, then, what thereat is, and this mystery
explore—
Let my heart be still a moment and this mystery
explore;—
   'Tis the wind and nothing more!"
Open here I flung the shutter, when, with many a flirt
and flutter,
In there stepped a stately Raven of the saintly days of
yore;
Not the least obeisance made he; not a minute stopped
or stayed he;
But, with mien of lord or lady, perched above my
chamber door—
Perched upon a bust of Pallas just above my chamber
door—
   Perched, and sat, and nothing more.
Then this ebony bird beguiling my sad fancy into
smiling,
By the grave and stern decorum of the countenance it
wore,

"Though thy crest be shorn and shaven, thou," I said,
"art sure no craven,
Ghastly grim and ancient Raven wandering from the
Nightly shore—
Tell me what thy lordly name is on the Night's
Plutonian shore!"
                Quoth the Raven "Nevermore."
Much I marvelled this ungainly fowl to hear discourse
so plainly,
Though its answer little meaning—little relevancy
bore;
For we cannot help agreeing that no living human
being
Ever yet was blest with seeing bird above his chamber
door—
Bird or beast upon the sculptured bust above his
chamber door,
                With such name as "Nevermore."
But the Raven, sitting lonely on the placid bust, spoke
only
That one word, as if his soul in that one word he did
outpour.
Nothing further then he uttered—not a feather then he
fluttered—
Till I scarcely more than muttered "Other friends have
flown before—
On the morrow *he* will leave me, as my hopes have
flown before."
                Then the bird said "Nevermore."
Startled at the stillness broken by reply so aptly
spoken,
"Doubtless," said I, "what it utters is its only stock
and store
Caught from some unhappy master whom unmerciful
Disaster

Followed fast and followed faster till his songs one
burden bore—
Till the dirges of his Hope that melancholy burden
bore
              Of 'Never—nevermore.'"
But the Raven still beguiling my sad fancy into
smiling,
Straight I wheeled a cushioned seat in front of bird,
and bust and door;
Then, upon the velvet sinking, I betook myself to
linking
Fancy unto fancy, thinking what this ominous bird of
yore—
What this grim, ungainly, ghastly, gaunt and ominous
bird of yore
              Meant in croaking "Nevermore."
This I sat engaged in guessing, but no syllable
expressing
To the fowl whose fiery eyes now burned into my
bosom's core;
This and more I sat divining, with my head at ease
reclining
On the cushion's velvet lining that the lamp-light
gloated o'er,
But whose velvet violet lining with the lamp-light
gloating o'er,
              She shall press, ah, nevermore!
Then, methought, the air grew denser, perfumed from
an unseen censer
Swung by Seraphim whose foot-falls tinkled on the
tufted floor.
"Wretch," I cried, "thy God hath lent thee—by these
angels he hath sent thee
Respite—respite and nepenthe, from thy memories of
Lenore;

Quaff, oh quaff this kind nepenthe and forget this lost
Lenore!"
       Quoth the Raven "Nevermore."
"Prophet!" said I, "thing of evil!—prophet still, if bird
or devil!—
Whether Tempter sent, or whether tempest tossed thee
here ashore,
Desolate yet all undaunted, on this desert land
enchanted—
On this home by Horror haunted—tell me truly, I
implore—
Is there—is there balm in Gilead?—tell me—tell me, I
implore!"
       Quoth the Raven "Nevermore."
"Prophet!" said I, "thing of evil—prophet still, if bird
or devil!
By that Heaven that bends above us—by that God we
both adore—
Tell this soul with sorrow laden if, within the distant
Aidenn,
It shall clasp a sainted maiden whom the angels name
Lenore—
Clasp a rare and radiant maiden whom the angels
name Lenore."
       Quoth the Raven "Nevermore."
"Be that word our sign in parting, bird or fiend!" I
shrieked, upstarting—
"Get thee back into the tempest and the Night's
Plutonian shore!
Leave no black plume as a token of that lie thy soul
hath spoken!
Leave my loneliness unbroken!—quit the bust above
my door!
Take thy beak from out my heart, and take thy form
from off my door!"

Quoth the Raven "Nevermore."
And the Raven, never flitting, still is sitting, *still* is
sitting
On the pallid bust of Pallas just above my chamber
door;
And his eyes have all the seeming of a demon's that is
dreaming,
And the lamp-light o'er him streaming throws his
shadow on the floor;
And my soul from out that shadow that lies floating on
the floor
Shall be lifted—nevermore!

The Murders in the Rue Morgue

THE mental features discoursed of as the analytical, are, in themselves, but little susceptible of analysis. We appreciate them only in their effects. We know of them, among other things, that they are always to their possessor, when inordinately possessed, a source of the liveliest enjoyment. As the strong man exults in his physical ability, delighting in such exercises as call his muscles into action, so glories the analyst in that moral activity which disentangles. He derives pleasure from even the most trivial occupations bringing his talent into play. He is fond of enigmas, of conundrums, of hieroglyphics; exhibiting in his solutions of each a degree of acumen which appears to the ordinary apprehension præternatural. His results, brought about by the very soul and essence of method, have, in truth, the whole air of intuition.

The faculty of re-solution is possibly much invigorated by mathematical study, and especially by that highest branch of it which, unjustly, and merely on account of its retrograde operations, has been called, as if par excellence, analysis. Yet to calculate is not in itself to analyse. A chess-player, for example, does the one without effort at the other. It follows that the game of chess, in its effects upon mental character, is greatly misunderstood. I am not now writing a treatise, but simply prefacing a somewhat peculiar narrative by observations very much at random; I will, therefore, take occasion to assert that the higher powers of the reflective intellect are more decidedly and more usefully tasked by the unostentatious game of draughts than by all the elaborate frivolity of chess. In this latter, where the pieces have different and bizarre motions, with various and variable values, what is only complex is mistaken (a not unusual error) for what is profound. The attention is here called powerfully into play. If it flag for an instant, an oversight is committed, resulting in injury or defeat. The possible moves being not only manifold but involute, the chances of such oversights are multiplied; and in nine cases out of ten it is the more concentrative rather than the more acute player who conquers. In draughts, on the contrary, where the moves are unique and have but little variation, the probabilities of inadvertence are diminished, and the mere attention being left comparatively unemployed, what advantages are obtained by either party are obtained by superior acumen. To be less abstract --Let us suppose a game of draughts where the pieces are reduced to four kings, and where, of course, no oversight is to be expected. It is obvious that here the victory can be decided (the players being at all equal) only by some recherche movement, the result of some strong exertion of the intellect. Deprived of ordinary resources, the analyst throws himself into the spirit of his opponent, identifies himself therewith, and not unfrequently sees thus, at a glance, the sole methods (sometimes indeed absurdly simple ones) by which he may seduce into error or hurry into miscalculation.

Whist has long been noted for its influence upon what is termed the calculating power; and men of the highest order of intellect have been known to take an apparently unaccountable delight in it, while eschewing chess as frivolous. Beyond doubt there is nothing of a similar nature so greatly tasking the faculty of analysis. The best chess-player in Christendom may be little more than the best player of chess; but proficiency in whist implies capacity for success in all those more important undertakings where mind struggles with mind. When I say proficiency, I mean that perfection in the game which includes a comprehension of all the sources whence legitimate advantage may be derived. These are not only manifold but multiform, and lie frequently among recesses of thought altogether inaccessible to the ordinary understanding. To observe attentively is to remember distinctly; and, so far, the concentrative chess-player will do very well at whist; while the rules of Hoyle (themselves based upon the mere mechanism of the game) are sufficiently and generally comprehensible. Thus to have a retentive memory, and to proceed by "the book," are points commonly regarded as the sum total of good playing. But it is in matters beyond the limits of mere rule that the skill of the analyst is evinced. He makes, in silence, a host of observations and inferences. So, perhaps, do his companions; and the difference in the extent of the information obtained, lies not so much in the validity of the inference as in the quality of the observation. The necessary knowledge is that of what to observe. Our player confines himself not at all; nor, because the game is the object, does he reject deductions from things external to the game. He examines the countenance of his partner, comparing it carefully with that of each of his opponents. He considers the mode of assorting the cards in each hand; often counting trump by trump, and honor by honor, through the glances bestowed by their holders upon each. He notes every variation of face as the play progresses, gathering a fund of thought from the differences in the expression of certainty, of surprise, of triumph, or of chagrin. From the manner of gathering up a trick he judges whether the person taking it can make another in the suit. He recognises what is played through feint, by the air with which it is thrown upon the table. A casual or inadvertent word; the accidental dropping or turning of a card, with the accompanying anxiety or carelessness in regard to its concealment; the counting of the tricks, with the order of their arrangement; embarrassment, hesitation, eagerness or trepidation --all afford, to his apparently intuitive perception, indications of the true state of affairs. The first two or three rounds having been played, he is in full possession of the contents of each hand, and thenceforward puts down his cards with as absolute a precision of purpose as if the rest of the party had turned outward the faces of their own.

The analytical power should not be confounded with simple ingenuity; for while the analyst is necessarily ingenious, the ingenious man is often remarkably incapable of analysis. The constructive or combining power, by which ingenuity is usually manifested, and to which the phrenologists (I believe erroneously) have assigned a separate organ, supposing it a primitive faculty, has been so frequently seen in those whose intellect bordered otherwise upon idiocy, as to have attracted general observation among writers on morals. Between ingenuity and the analytic ability there exists a difference far greater, indeed, than that between the fancy and the imagination, but of a character very strictly analogous. It will be found, in fact, that the ingenious are always fanciful, and the truly imaginative never otherwise than analytic.

The narrative which follows will appear to the reader somewhat in the light of a commentary upon the propositions just advanced.

Residing in Paris during the spring and part of the summer of 18--, I there became acquainted with a Monsieur C. Auguste Dupin. This young gentleman was of an excellent -- indeed of an illustrious family, but, by a variety of untoward events, had been reduced to such poverty that the energy of his character succumbed beneath it, and he ceased to bestir himself in the world, or to care for the retrieval of his fortunes. By courtesy of his creditors, there still remained in his possession a small remnant of his patrimony; and, upon the income arising from this, he managed, by means of a rigorous economy, to procure the necessaries of life, without troubling himself about its superfluities. Books, indeed, were his sole luxuries, and in Paris these are easily obtained.

Our first meeting was at an obscure library in the Rue Montmartre, where the accident of our both being in search of the same very rare and very remarkable volume, brought us into closer communion. We saw each other again and again. I was deeply interested in the little family history which he detailed to me with all that candor which a Frenchman indulges whenever mere self is his theme. I was astonished, too, at the vast extent of his reading; and, above all, I felt my soul enkindled within me by the wild fervor, and the vivid freshness of his imagination. Seeking in Paris the objects I then sought, I felt that the society of such a man would be to me a treasure beyond price; and this feeling I frankly confided to him. It was at length arranged that we should live together during my stay in the city; and as my worldly circumstances were somewhat less embarrassed than his own, I was permitted to be at the expense of renting, and furnishing in a style which suited the rather fantastic gloom of our common temper, a time-eaten and grotesque mansion, long deserted through superstitions into which we did not inquire, and tottering to its fall in a retired and desolate portion of the Faubourg St. Germain.

Had the routine of our life at this place been known to the world, we should have been regarded as madmen --although, perhaps, as madmen of a harmless nature. Our seclusion was perfect. We admitted no visitors. Indeed the locality of our retirement had been carefully kept a secret from my own former associates; and it had been many years since Dupin had ceased to know or be known in Paris. We existed within ourselves alone.

It was a freak of fancy in my friend (for what else shall I call it?) to be enamored of the Night for her own sake; and into this bizarrerie, as into all his others, I quietly fell; giving myself up to his wild whims with a perfect abandon. The sable divinity would not herself dwell with us always; but we could counterfeit her presence. At the first dawn of the morning we closed all the messy shutters of our old building; lighting a couple of tapers which, strongly perfumed, threw out only the ghastliest and feeblest of rays. By the aid of these we then busied our souls in dreams --reading, writing, or conversing, until warned by the clock of the advent of the true Darkness. Then we sallied forth into the streets, arm in arm, continuing the topics of the day, or roaming far and wide until a late hour, seeking, amid the wild lights and shadows of the populous city, that infinity of mental excitement which quiet observation can afford.

At such times I could not help remarking and admiring (although from his rich ideality I had been prepared to expect it) a peculiar analytic ability in Dupin. He seemed, too, to take an eager delight in its exercise --if not exactly in its display --and did not hesitate to confess the pleasure thus derived. He boasted to me, with a low chuckling laugh, that most men, in respect to himself, wore windows in their bosoms, and was wont to follow up such assertions by direct and very startling proofs of his intimate knowledge of my own. His manner at these moments was frigid and abstract; his eyes were vacant in expression; while his voice, usually a rich tenor, rose into a treble which would have sounded petulantly but for the deliberateness and entire distinctness of the enunciation. Observing him in these moods, I often dwelt meditatively upon the old philosophy of the Bi-Part Soul, and amused myself with the fancy of a double Dupin --the creative and the resolvent.

Let it not be supposed, from what I have just said, that I am detailing any mystery, or penning any romance. What I have described in the Frenchman, was merely the result of an excited, or perhaps of a diseased intelligence. But of the character of his remarks at the periods in question an example will best convey the idea.

We were strolling one night down a long dirty street, in the vicinity of the Palais Royal. Being both, apparently, occupied with thought, neither of us had spoken a syllable for fifteen minutes at least. All at once Dupin broke forth with these words:

"He is a very little fellow, that's true, and would do better for the Théâtre des Variétés."

"There can be no doubt of that," I replied unwittingly, and not at first observing (so much had I been absorbed in reflection) the extraordinary manner in which the speaker had chimed in with my meditations. In an instant afterward I recollected myself, and my astonishment was profound.

"Dupin," said I, gravely, "this is beyond my comprehension. I do not hesitate to say that I am amazed, and can scarcely credit my senses. How was it possible you should know I was thinking of _____ ?" Here I paused, to ascertain beyond a doubt whether he really knew of whom I thought.

_____ "of Chantilly," said he, "why do you pause? You were remarking to yourself that his diminutive figure unfitted him for tragedy."

This was precisely what had formed the subject of my reflections. Chantilly was a quondam cobbler of the Rue St. Denis, who, becoming stage-mad, had attempted the rôle of Xerxes, in Crébillon's tragedy so called, and been notoriously Pasquinaded for his pains.

"Tell me, for Heaven's sake," I exclaimed, "the method --if method there is --by which you have been enabled to fathom my soul in this matter." In fact I was even more startled than I would have been willing to express.

"It was the fruiterer," replied my friend, "who brought you to the conclusion that the mender of soles was not of sufficient height for Xerxes et id genus omne."

"The fruiterer! --you astonish me --I know no fruiterer whomsoever."

"The man who ran up against you as we entered the street --it may have been fifteen minutes ago."

I now remembered that, in fact, a fruiterer, carrying upon his head a large basket of apples, had nearly thrown me down, by accident, as we passed from the Rue C_____ into the thoroughfare where we stood; but what this had to do with Chantilly I could not possibly understand.

There was not a particle of charlatanerie about Dupin. "I will explain," he said, "and that you may comprehend all clearly, we will first retrace the course of your meditations, from the moment in which I spoke to you until that of the rencontre with the fruiterer in question. The larger links of the chain run thus --Chantilly, Orion, Dr. Nichols, Epicurus, Stereotomy, the street stones, the fruiterer."

There are few persons who have not, at some period of their lives, amused themselves in retracing the steps by which particular conclusions of their own minds have been attained. The occupation is often full of interest; and he who attempts it for the first time is astonished by the apparently illimitable distance and incoherence between the starting-point and the goal. What, then, must have been my amazement when I heard the Frenchman speak what he had just spoken, and when I could not help acknowledging that he had spoken the truth. He continued:

"We had been talking of horses, if I remember aright, just before leaving the Rue C_____. This was the last subject we discussed. As we crossed into this street, a fruiterer, with a large basket upon his head, brushing quickly past us, thrust you upon a pile of paving-stones collected at a spot where the causeway is undergoing repair. You stepped upon one of the loose fragments, slipped, slightly strained your ankle, appeared vexed or sulky, muttered a few words, turned to look at the pile, and then proceeded in silence. I was not particularly attentive to what you did; but observation has become with me, of late, a species of necessity.

"You kept your eyes upon the ground --glancing, with a petulant expression, at the holes and ruts in the pavement, (so that I saw you were still thinking of the stones,) until we reached the little alley called Lamartine, which has been paved, by way of experiment, with the overlapping and riveted blocks. Here your countenance brightened up, and, perceiving your lips move, I could not doubt that you murmured the word 'stereotomy,' a term very affectedly applied to this species of pavement. I knew that you could not say to yourself 'stereotomy' without being brought to think of atomies, and thus of the theories of Epicurus; and since, when we discussed this subject not very long ago, I mentioned to you how singularly, yet with how little notice, the vague guesses of that noble Greek had met with confirmation in the late nebular cosmogony, I felt that you could not avoid casting your eyes upward to the great nebula in Orion, and I certainly expected that you would do so. You did look up; and I was now assured that I had correctly followed your steps. But in that bitter tirade upon Chantilly, which appeared in yesterday's 'Musée,' the satirist, making some disgraceful allusions to the cobbler's change of name upon assuming the buskin,

quoted a Latin line about which we have often
conversed. I mean the line

Perdidit antiquum litera prima
sonum

I had told you that this was in reference to Orion,
formerly written Urion; and, from certain pungencies
connected with this explanation, I was aware that you
could not have forgotten it. It was clear, therefore, that
you would not fail to combine the two ideas of Orion
and Chantilly. That you did combine them I saw by the
character of the smile which passed over your lips. You
thought of the poor cobbler's immolation. So far, you
had been stooping in your gait; but now I saw you
draw yourself up to your full height. I was then sure
that you reflected upon the diminutive figure of
Chantilly. At this point I interrupted your meditations
to remark that as, in fact, he was a very little fellow --
that Chantilly --he would do better at the Théâtre des
Variétés."

Not long after this, we were looking over an evening
edition of the "Gazette des Tribunaux," when the
following paragraphs arrested our attention.

"EXTRAORDINARY MURDERS. --This morning,
about three o'clock, the inhabitants of the Quartier St.
Roch were aroused from sleep by a succession of
terrific shrieks, issuing, apparently, from the fourth
story of a house in the Rue Morgue, known to be in the
sole occupancy of one Madame L'Espanaye, and her
daughter, Mademoiselle Camille L'Espanaye. After
some delay, occasioned by a fruitless attempt to
procure admission in the usual manner, the gateway
was broken in with a crowbar, and eight or ten of the
neighbors entered, accompanied by two gendarmes. By
this time the cries had ceased; but, as the party rushed
up the first flight of stairs, two or more rough voices,

in angry contention, were distinguished, and seemed
to proceed from the upper part of the house. As the
second landing was reached, these sounds, also, had
ceased, and everything remained perfectly quiet. The
party spread themselves, and hurried from room to
room. Upon arriving at a large back chamber in the
fourth story, (the door of which, being found locked,
with the key inside, was forced open,) a spectacle
presented itself which struck every one present not
less with horror than with astonishment.

"The apartment was in the wildest disorder --the
furniture broken and thrown about in all directions.
There was only one bedstead; and from this the bed
had been removed, and thrown into the middle of the
floor. On a chair lay a razor, besmeared with blood. On
the hearth were two or three long and thick tresses of
grey human hair, also dabbled in blood, and seeming
to have been pulled out by the roots. Upon the floor
were found four Napoleons, an ear-ring of topaz, three
large silver spoons, three smaller of métal d'Alger, and
two bags, containing nearly four thousand francs in
gold. The drawers of a bureau, which stood in one
corner, were open, and had been, apparently, rifled,
although many articles still remained in them. A small
iron safe was discovered under the bed (not under the
bedstead). It was open, with the key still in the door. It
had no contents beyond a few old letters, and other
papers of little consequence.

"Of Madame L'Espanaye no traces were here seen;
but an unusual quantity of soot being observed in the
fire-place, a search was made in the chimney, and
(horrible to relate!) the corpse of the daughter, head
downward, was dragged therefrom; it having been
thus forced up the narrow aperture for a considerable
distance. The body was quite warm. Upon examining

it, many excoriations were perceived, no doubt occasioned by the violence with which it had been thrust up and disengaged. Upon the face were many severe scratches, and, upon the throat, dark bruises, and deep indentations of finger nails, as if the deceased had been throttled to death.

"After a thorough investigation of every portion of the house, without farther discovery, the party made its way into a small paved yard in the rear of the building, where lay the corpse of the old lady, with her throat so entirely cut that, upon an attempt to raise her, the head fell off. The body, as well as the head, was fearfully mutilated --the former so much so as scarcely to retain any semblance of humanity.

"To this horrible mystery there is not as yet, we believe, the slightest clew."

The next day's paper had these additional particulars.

"The Tragedy in the Rue Morgue. Many individuals have been examined in relation to this most extraordinary and frightful affair." [The word 'affaire' has not yet, in France, that levity of import which it conveys with us,] "but nothing whatever has transpired to throw light upon it. We give below all the material testimony elicited.

"Pauline Dubourg, laundress, deposes that she has known both the deceased for three years, having washed for them during that period. The old lady and her daughter seemed on good terms --very affectionate towards each other. They were excellent pay. Could not speak in regard to their mode or means of living. Believed that Madame L. told fortunes for a living. Was reputed to have money put by. Never met any persons in the house when she called for the clothes or took them home. Was sure that they had no servant in employ. There appeared to be no furniture in any part of the building except in the fourth story.

"Pierre Moreau, tobacconist, deposes that he has been in the habit of selling small quantities of tobacco and snuff to Madame L'Espanaye for nearly four years. Was born in the neighborhood, and has always resided there. The deceased and her daughter had occupied the house in which the corpses were found, for more than six years. It was formerly occupied by a jeweller, who under-let the upper rooms to various persons. The house was the property of Madame L. She became dissatisfied with the abuse of the premises by her tenant, and moved into them herself, refusing to let any portion. The old lady was childish. Witness had seen the daughter some five or six times during the six years. The two lived an exceedingly retired life --were reputed to have money. Had heard it said among the neighbors that Madame L. told fortunes --did not believe it. Had never seen any person enter the door except the old lady and her daughter, a porter once or twice, and a physician some eight or ten times.

"Many other persons, neighbors, gave evidence to the same effect. No one was spoken of as frequenting the house. It was not known whether there were any living connexions of Madame L. and her daughter. The shutters of the front windows were seldom opened. Those in the rear were always closed, with the exception of the large back room, fourth story. The house was a good house --not very old.

"Isidore Musèt, gendarme, deposes that he was called to the house about three o'clock in the morning, and found some twenty or thirty persons at the gateway, endeavoring to gain admittance. Forced it open, at length, with a bayonet --not with a crowbar. Had but little difficulty in getting it open, on account of its being a double or folding gate, and bolted neither at bottom nor top. The shrieks were continued until the gate was forced --and then suddenly ceased. They seemed to be screams of some person (or persons) in great agony --were loud and drawn out, not short and quick. Witness led the way up stairs. Upon reaching the first landing, heard two voices in loud and angry contention --the one a gruff voice, the other much shriller --a very strange voice. Could distinguish some words of the former, which was that of a Frenchman. Was positive that it was not a woman's voice. Could distinguish the words 'sacré' and 'diable.' The shrill voice was that of a foreigner. Could not be sure whether it was the voice of a man or of a woman. Could not make out what was said, but believed the language to be Spanish. The state of the room and of the bodies was described by this witness as we described them yesterday.

"Henri Duval, a neighbor, and by trade a silver-smith, deposes that he was one of the party who first entered the house. Corroborates the testimony of Musèt in general. As soon as they forced an entrance, they reclosed the door, to keep out the crowd, which collected very fast, notwithstanding the lateness of the hour. The shrill voice, this witness thinks, was that of an Italian. Was certain it was not French. Could not be sure that it was a man's voice. It might have been a woman's. Was not acquainted with the Italian language. Could not distinguish the words, but was convinced by the intonation that the speaker was an Italian. Knew Madame L. and her daughter. Had conversed with both frequently. Was sure that the shrill voice was not that of either of the deceased.

"_____ Odenheimer, restaurateur. This witness volunteered his testimony. Not speaking French, was examined through an interpreter. Is a native of Amsterdam. Was passing the house at the time of the shrieks. They lasted for several minutes --probably ten. They were long and loud --very awful and distressing. Was one of those who entered the building. Corroborated the previous evidence in every respect but one. Was sure that the shrill voice was that of a man --of a Frenchman. Could not distinguish the words uttered. They were loud and quick --unequal -- spoken apparently in fear as well as in anger. The voice was harsh --not so much shrill as harsh. Could not call it a shrill voice. The gruff voice said repeatedly 'sacré,' 'diable,' and once 'mon Dieu.'

"Jules Mignaud, banker, of the firm of Mignaud et Fils, Rue Deloraine. Is the elder Mignaud. Madame L'Espanaye had some property. Had opened an account with his banking house in the spring of the year ---- (eight years previously). Made frequent deposits in small sums. Had checked for nothing until the third day before her death, when she took out in person the sum of 4000 francs. This sum was paid in gold, and a clerk went home with the money.

"Adolphe Le Bon, clerk to Mignaud et Fils, deposes that on the day in question, about noon, he accompanied Madame L'Espanaye to her residence with the 4000 francs, put up in two bags. Upon the door being opened, Mademoiselle L. appeared and took from his hands one of the bags, while the old lady relieved him of the other. He then bowed and departed. Did not see any person in the street at the time. It is a bye-street --very lonely.

"William Bird, tailor deposes that he was one of the party who entered the house. Is an Englishman. Has lived in Paris two years. Was one of the first to ascend the stairs. Heard the voices in contention. The gruff voice was that of a Frenchman. Could make out several words, but cannot now remember all. Heard distinctly 'sacré' and 'mon Dieu.' There was a sound at the moment as if of several persons struggling --a scraping and scuffling sound. The shrill voice was very loud --louder than the gruff one. Is sure that it was not the voice of an Englishman. Appeared to be that of a German. Might have been a woman's voice. Does not understand German.

"Four of the above-named witnesses, being recalled, deposed that the door of the chamber in which was found the body of Mademoiselle L. was locked on the inside when the party reached it. Every thing was perfectly silent --no groans or noises of any kind. Upon forcing the door no person was seen. The windows, both of the back and front room, were down and firmly fastened from within. A door between the two rooms was closed, but not locked. The door leading from the front room into the passage was locked, with the key on the inside. A small room in the front of the house, on the fourth story, at the head of the passage, was open, the door being ajar. This room was crowded with old beds, boxes, and so forth. These were carefully removed and searched. There was not an inch of any portion of the house which was not carefully searched. Sweeps were sent up and down the chimneys. The house was a four story one, with garrets (mansardes.) A trap-door on the roof was nailed down very securely --did not appear to have been opened for years. The time elapsing between the hearing of the voices in contention and the breaking open of the room door, was variously stated by the witnesses. Some made it as short as three minutes -- some as long as five. The door was opened with difficulty.

"Alfonzo Garcio, undertaker, deposes that he resides
in the Rue Morgue. Is a native of Spain. Was one of the
party who entered the house. Did not proceed up
stairs. Is nervous, and was apprehensive of the
consequences of agitation. Heard the voices in
contention. The gruff voice was that of a Frenchman.
Could not distinguish what was said. The shrill voice
was that of an Englishman --is sure of this. Does not
understand the English language, but judges by the
intonation.

"Alberto Montani, confectioner, deposes that he was
among the first to ascend the stairs. Heard the voices
in question. The gruff voice was that of a Frenchman.
Distinguished several words. The speaker appeared to
be expostulating. Could not make out the words of the
shrill voice. Spoke quick and unevenly. Thinks it the
voice of a Russian. Corroborates the general testimony.
Is an Italian. Never conversed with a native of Russia.

"Several witnesses, recalled, here testified that the
chimneys of all the rooms on the fourth story were too
narrow to admit the passage of a human being. By
'sweeps' were meant cylindrical sweeping-brushes,
such as are employed by those who clean chimneys.
These brushes were passed up and down every flue in
the house. There is no back passage by which any one
could have descended while the party proceeded up
stairs. The body of Mademoiselle L'Espanaye was so
firmly wedged in the chimney that it could not be got
down until four or five of the party united their
strength.

"Paul Dumas, physician, deposes that he was called
to view the bodies about day-break. They were both
then lying on the sacking of the bedstead in the
chamber where Mademoiselle L. was found. The corpse
of the young lady was much bruised and excoriated.

The fact that it had been thrust up the chimney would sufficiently account for these appearances. The throat was greatly chafed. There were several deep scratches just below the chin, together with a series of livid spots which were evidently the impression of fingers. The face was fearfully discolored, and the eye-balls protruded. The tongue had been partially bitten through. A large bruise was discovered upon the pit of the stomach, produced, apparently, by the pressure of a knee. In the opinion of M. Dumas, Mademoiselle L'Espanaye had been throttled to death by some person or persons unknown. The corpse of the mother was horribly mutilated. All the bones of the right leg and arm were more or less shattered. The left tibia much splintered, as well as all the ribs of the left side. Whole body dreadfully bruised and discolored. It was not possible to say how the injuries had been inflicted. A heavy club of wood, or a broad bar of iron --a chair -- any large, heavy, and obtuse weapon would have produced such results, if wielded by the hands of a very powerful man. No woman could have inflicted the blows with any weapon. The head of the deceased, when seen by witness, was entirely separated from the body, and was also greatly shattered. The throat had evidently been cut with some very sharp instrument --probably with a razor.

"Alexandre Etienne, surgeon, was called with M. Dumas to view the bodies. Corroborated the testimony, and the opinions of M. Dumas.

"Nothing farther of importance was elicited, although several other persons were examined. A murder so mysterious, and so perplexing in all its particulars, was never before committed in Paris --if indeed a murder has been committed at all. The police are entirely at fault --an unusual occurrence in affairs

of this nature. There is not, however, the shadow of a
clew apparent."

The evening edition of the paper stated that the
greatest excitement still continued in the Quartier St.
Roch --that the premises in question had been
carefully re-searched, and fresh examinations of
witnesses instituted, but all to no purpose. A
postscript, however, mentioned that Adolphe Le Bon
had been arrested and imprisoned --although nothing
appeared to criminate him, beyond the facts already
detailed.

Dupin seemed singularly interested in the progress
of this affair --at least so I judged from his manner,
for he made no comments. It was only after the
announcement that Le Bon had been imprisoned, that
he asked me my opinion respecting the murders.

I could merely agree with all Paris in considering
them an insoluble mystery. I saw no means by which it
would be possible to trace the murderer.

"We must not judge of the means," said Dupin, "by
this shell of an examination. The Parisian police, so
much extolled for acumen, are cunning, but no more.
There is no method in their proceedings, beyond the
method of the moment. They make a vast parade of
measures; but, not unfrequently, these are so ill
adapted to the objects proposed, as to put us in mind
of Monsieur Jourdain's calling for his robe-de-
chambre --pour mieux entendre la musique. The
results attained by them are not unfrequently
surprising, but, for the most part, are brought about by
simple diligence and activity. When these qualities are
unavailing, their schemes fail. Vidocq, for example,
was a good guesser, and a persevering man. But,
without educated thought, he erred continually by the
very intensity of his investigations. He impaired his

vision by holding the object too close. He might see, perhaps, one or two points with unusual clearness, but in so doing he, necessarily, lost sight of the matter as a whole. Thus there is such a thing as being too profound. Truth is not always in a well. In fact, as regards the more important knowledge, I do believe that she is invariably superficial. The depth lies in the valleys where we seek her, and not upon the mountain-tops where she is found. The modes and sources of this kind of error are well typified in the contemplation of the heavenly bodies. To look at a star by glances --to view it in a side-long way, by turning toward it the exterior portions of the retina (more susceptible of feeble impressions of light than the interior), is to behold the star distinctly -- is to have the best appreciation of its lustre --a lustre which grows dim just in proportion as we turn our vision fully upon it. A greater number of rays actually fall upon the eye in the latter case, but, in the former, there is the more refined capacity for comprehension. By undue profundity we perplex and enfeeble thought; and it is possible to make even Venus herself vanish from the firmanent by a scrutiny too sustained, too concentrated, or too direct.

"As for these murders, let us enter into some examinations for ourselves, before we make up an opinion respecting them. An inquiry will afford us amusement," (I thought this an odd term, so applied, but said nothing) "and, besides, Le Bon once rendered me a service for which I am not ungrateful. We will go and see the premises with our own eyes. I know G____, the Prefect of Police, and shall have no difficulty in obtaining the necessary permission."

The permission was obtained, and we proceeded at once to the Rue Morgue. This is one of those miserable thoroughfares which intervene between the Rue Richelieu and the Rue St. Roch. It was late in the afternoon when we reached it; as this quarter is at a great distance from that in which we resided. The house was readily found; for there were still many persons gazing up at the closed shutters, with an objectless curiosity, from the opposite side of the way. It was an ordinary Parisian house, with a gateway, on one side of which was a glazed watch-box, with a sliding panel in the window, indicating a loge de concierge. Before going in we walked up the street, turned down an alley, and then, again turning, passed in the rear of the building --Dupin, meanwhile, examining the whole neighborhood, as well as the house, with a minuteness of attention for which I could see no possible object.

Retracing our steps, we came again to the front of the dwelling, rang, and, having shown our credentials, were admitted by the agents in charge. We went up stairs --into the chamber where the body of Mademoiselle L'Espanaye had been found, and where both the deceased still lay. The disorders of the room had, as usual, been suffered to exist. I saw nothing beyond what had been stated in the "Gazette des Tribunaux." Dupin scrutinized every thing --not excepting the bodies of the victims. We then went into the other rooms, and into the yard; a gendarme accompanying us throughout. The examination occupied us until dark, when we took our departure. On our way home my companion stepped in for a moment at the office of one of the daily papers.

I have said that the whims of my friend were manifold, and that Je les ménagais: --for this phrase there is no English equivalent. It was his humor, now, to decline all conversation on the subject of the murder, until about noon the next day. He then asked me, suddenly, if I had observed any thing peculiar at the scene of the atrocity.

There was something in his manner of emphasizing the word "peculiar," which caused me to shudder, without knowing why.

"No, nothing peculiar," I said; "nothing more, at least, than we both saw stated in the paper."

"The 'Gazette,' " he replied, "has not entered, I fear, into the unusual horror of the thing. But dismiss the idle opinions of this print. It appears to me that this mystery is considered insoluble, for the very reason which should cause it to be regarded as easy of solution --I mean for the outré character of its features. The police are confounded by the seeming absence of motive --not for the murder itself --but for the atrocity of the murder. They are puzzled, too, by the seeming impossibility of reconciling the voices heard in contention, with the facts that no one was discovered up stairs but the assassinated Mademoiselle L'Espanaye, and that there were no means of egress without the notice of the party ascending. The wild disorder of the room; the corpse thrust, with the head downward, up the chimney; the frightful mutilation of the body of the old lady; these considerations, with those just mentioned, and others which I need not mention, have sufficed to paralyze the powers, by putting completely at fault the boasted acumen, of the government agents. They have fallen into the gross but common error of confounding the unusual with the abstruse. But it is by these deviations from the plane of the ordinary, that reason feels its way, if at all, in its search for the true. In investigations such as we are now pursuing, it should not be so much asked 'what has occurred,' as 'what has occurred that has never occurred before.' In fact, the facility with which I shall arrive, or have arrived, at the solution of this mystery, is in the direct ratio of its apparent insolubility in the eyes of the police."

I stared at the speaker in mute astonishment.

"I am now awaiting," continued he, looking toward the door of our apartment --"I am now awaiting a person who, although perhaps not the perpetrator of these butcheries, must have been in some measure implicated in their perpetration. Of the worst portion of the crimes committed, it is probable that he is innocent. I hope that I am right in this supposition; for upon it I build my expectation of reading the entire riddle. I look for the man here --in this room --every moment. It is true that he may not arrive; but the probability is that he will. Should he come, it will be necessary to detain him. Here are pistols; and we both know how to use them when occasion demands their use."

I took the pistols, scarcely knowing what I did, or believing what I heard, while Dupin went on, very much as if in a soliloquy. I have already spoken of his abstract manner at such times. His discourse was addressed to myself; but his voice, although by no means loud, had that intonation which is commonly employed in speaking to some one at a great distance. His eyes, vacant in expression, regarded only the wall.

"That the voices heard in contention," he said, "by the party upon the stairs, were not the voices of the women themselves, was fully proved by the evidence. This relieves us of all doubt upon the question whether the old lady could have first destroyed the daughter, and afterward have committed suicide. I speak of this point chiefly for the sake of method; for the strength of Madame L'Espanaye would have been utterly unequal to the task of thrusting her daughter's corpse up the chimney as it was found; and the nature of the wounds upon her own person entirely preclude the idea of self-destruction. Murder, then, has been committed by some third party; and the voices of this third party were those heard in contention. Let me now advert --not to the whole testimony respecting these voices --but to what was peculiar in that testimony. Did you observe any thing peculiar about it?"

I remarked that, while all the witnesses agreed in supposing the gruff voice to be that of a Frenchman, there was much disagreement in regard to the shrill, or, as one individual termed it, the harsh voice.

"That was the evidence itself," said Dupin, "but it was not the peculiarity of the evidence. You have observed nothing distinctive. Yet there was something to be observed. The witnesses, as you remark, agreed about the gruff voice; they were here unanimous. But in regard to the shrill voice, the peculiarity is --not that they disagreed --but that, while an Italian, an Englishman, a Spaniard, a Hollander, and a Frenchman attempted to describe it, each one spoke of it as that of a foreigner. Each is sure that it was not the voice of one of his own countrymen. Each likens it -- not to the voice of an individual of any nation with whose language he is conversant --but the converse. The Frenchman supposes it the voice of a Spaniard, and 'might have distinguished some words had he been acquainted with the Spanish.' The Dutchman maintains it to have been that of a Frenchman; but we find it stated that 'not understanding French this witness was examined through an interpreter.' The Englishman thinks it the voice of a German, and 'does not understand German.' The Spaniard 'is sure' that it

was that of an Englishman, but 'judges by the
intonation' altogether, 'as he has no knowledge of the
English.' The Italian believes it the voice of a Russian,
but 'has never conversed with a native of Russia.' A
second Frenchman differs, moreover, with the first,
and is positive that the voice was that of an Italian;
but, not being cognizant of that tongue, is, like the
Spaniard, 'convinced by the intonation.' Now, how
strangely unusual must that voice have really been,
about which such testimony as this could have been
elicited! --in whose tones, even, denizens of the five
great divisions of Europe could recognise nothing
familiar! You will say that it might have been the voice
of an Asiatic --of an African. Neither Asiatics nor
Africans abound in Paris; but, without denying the
inference, I will now merely call your attention to
three points. The voice is termed by one witness 'harsh
rather than shrill.' It is represented by two others to
have been 'quick and unequal.' No words --no sounds
resembling words --were by any witness mentioned
as distinguishable.

"I know not," continued Dupin, "what impression I
may have made, so far, upon your own understanding;
but I do not hesitate to say that legitimate deductions
even from this portion of the testimony --the portion
respecting the gruff and shrill voices --are in
themselves sufficient to engender a suspicion which
should give direction to all farther progress in the
investigation of the mystery. I said 'legitimate
deductions;' but my meaning is not thus fully
expressed. I designed to imply that the deductions are
the sole proper ones, and that the suspicion arises
inevitably from them as the single result. What the
suspicion is, however, I will not say just yet. I merely
wish you to bear in mind that, with myself, it was

sufficiently forcible to give a definite form --a certain tendency --to my inquiries in the chamber.

"Let us now transport ourselves, in fancy, to this chamber. What shall we first seek here? The means of egress employed by the murderers. It is not too much to say that neither of us believe in praeternatural events. Madame and Mademoiselle L'Espanaye were not destroyed by spirits. The doers of the deed were material, and escaped materially. Then how? Fortunately, there is but one mode of reasoning upon the point, and that mode must lead us to a definite decision. --Let us examine, each by each, the possible means of egress. It is clear that the assassins were in the room where Mademoiselle L'Espanaye was found, or at least in the room adjoining, when the party ascended the stairs. It is then only from these two apartments that we have to seek issues. The police have laid bare the floors, the ceilings, and the masonry of the walls, in every direction. No secret issues could have escaped their vigilance. But, not trusting to their eyes, I examined with my own. There were, then, no secret issues. Both doors leading from the rooms into the passage were securely locked, with the keys inside. Let us turn to the chimneys. These, although of ordinary width for some eight or ten feet above the hearths, will not admit, throughout their extent, the body of a large cat. The impossibility of egress, by means already stated, being thus absolute, we are reduced to the windows. Through those of the front room no one could have escaped without notice from the crowd in the street. The murderers must have passed, then, through those of the back room. Now, brought to this conclusion in so unequivocal a manner as we are, it is not our part, as reasoners, to reject it on account of apparent impossibilities. It is only left for us to prove that these apparent 'impossibilities' are, in reality, not such.

"There are two windows in the chamber. One of them is unobstructed by furniture, and is wholly visible. The lower portion of the other is hidden from view by the head of the unwieldy bedstead which is thrust close up against it. The former was found securely fastened from within. It resisted the utmost force of those who endeavored to raise it. A large gimlet-hole had been pierced in its frame to the left, and a very stout nail was found fitted therein, nearly to the head. Upon examining the other window, a similar nail was seen similarly fitted in it; and a vigorous attempt to raise this sash, failed also. The police were now entirely satisfied that egress had not been in these directions. And, therefore, it was thought a matter of supererogation to withdraw the nails and open the windows.

"My own examination was somewhat more particular, and was so for the reason I have just given --because here it was, I knew, that all apparent impossibilities must be proved to be not such in reality.

"I proceeded to think thus --à posteriori. The murderers did escape from one of these windows. This being so, they could not have re-fastened the sashes from the inside, as they were found fastened; --the consideration which put a stop, through its obviousness, to the scrutiny of the police in this quarter. Yet the sashes were fastened. They must, then, have the power of fastening themselves. There was no escape from this conclusion. I stepped to the unobstructed casement, withdrew the nail with some difficulty, and attempted to raise the sash. It resisted all my efforts, as I had anticipated. A concealed spring must, I now knew, exist; and this corroboration of my idea convinced me that my premises, at least, were correct, however mysterious still appeared the circumstances attending the nails. A careful search soon brought to light the hidden spring. I pressed it, and, satisfied with the discovery, forbore to upraise the sash.

"I now replaced the nail and regarded it attentively. A person passing out through this window might have reclosed it, and the spring would have caught --but the nail could not have been replaced. The conclusion was plain, and again narrowed in the field of my investigations. The assassins must have escaped through the other window. Supposing, then, the springs upon each sash to be the same, as was probable, there must be found a difference between the nails, or at least between the modes of their fixture. Getting upon the sacking of the bedstead, I looked over the head-board minutely at the second casement. Passing my hand down behind the board, I readily discovered and pressed the spring, which was, as I had supposed, identical in character with its neighbor. I now looked at the nail. It was as stout as the other, and apparently fitted in the same manner --driven in nearly up to the head.

"You will say that I was puzzled; but, if you think so, you must have misunderstood the nature of the inductions. To use a sporting phrase, I had not been once 'at fault.' The scent had never for an instant been lost. There was no flaw in any link of the chain. I had traced the secret to its ultimate result, --and that result was the nail. It had, I say, in every respect, the appearance of its fellow in the other window; but this fact was an absolute nullity (conclusive as it might seem to be) when compared with the consideration that here, at this point, terminated the clew. 'There must be something wrong,' I said, 'about the nail.' I touched it; and the head, with about a quarter of an inch of the shank, came off in my fingers. The rest of the shank was in the gimlet-hole, where it had been broken off. The fracture was an old one (for its edges were incrusted with rust), and had apparently been accomplished by the blow of a hammer, which had partially imbedded, in the top of the bottom sash, the head portion of the nail. I now carefully replaced this head portion in the indentation whence I had taken it, and the resemblance to a perfect nail was complete -- the fissure was invisible. Pressing the spring, I gently raised the sash for a few inches; the head went up with it, remaining firm in its bed. I closed the window, and the semblance of the whole nail was again perfect.

"The riddle, so far, was now unriddled. The assassin had escaped through the window which looked upon the bed. Dropping of its own accord upon his exit (or perhaps purposely closed), it had become fastened by the spring; and it was the retention of this spring which had been mistaken by the police for that of the nail, --farther inquiry being thus considered unnecessary.

"The next question is that of the mode of descent. Upon this point I had been satisfied in my walk with you around the building. About five feet and a half from the casement in question there runs a lightning-rod. From this rod it would have been impossible for any one to reach the window itself, to say nothing of entering it. I observed, however, that the shutters of the fourth story were of the peculiar kind called by Parisian carpenters ferrades --a kind rarely employed at the present day, but frequently seen upon very old mansions at Lyons and Bourdeaux. They are in the form of an ordinary door, (a single, not a folding door) except that the lower half is latticed or worked in open trellis --thus affording an excellent hold for the hands. In the present instance these shutters are fully three feet and a half broad. When we saw them from the rear of the house, they were both about half open --that is to say, they stood off at right angles from the wall. It is probable that the police, as well as myself, examined the back of the tenement; but, if so, in looking at these ferrades in the line of their breadth (as they must have done), they did not perceive this great breadth itself, or, at all events, failed to take it into due consideration. In fact, having once satisfied themselves that no egress could have been made in this quarter, they would naturally bestow here a very cursory examination. It was clear to me, however, that the shutter belonging to the window at the head of the bed, would, if swung fully back to the wall, reach to within two feet of the lightning-rod. It was also evident that, by exertion of a very unusual degree of activity and courage, an entrance into the window, from the rod, might have been thus effected. --By reaching to the distance of two feet and a half (we now suppose the shutter open to its whole extent) a robber might have taken a firm grasp upon the trellis-work. Letting go, then, his hold upon the rod, placing his feet securely against the wall, and springing boldly from it, he might have swung the shutter so as to close it, and, if we imagine the window open at the time, might even have swung himself into the room.

"I wish you to bear especially in mind that I have spoken of a very unusual degree of activity as requisite to success in so hazardous and so difficult a feat. It is my design to show you, first, that the thing might possibly have been accomplished: --but, secondly and chiefly, I wish to impress upon your understanding the very extraordinary --the almost præternatural character of that agility which could have accomplished it.

"You will say, no doubt, using the language of the law, that 'to make out my case,' I should rather undervalue, than insist upon a full estimation of the activity required in this matter. This may be the practice in law, but it is not the usage of reason. My ultimate object is only the truth. My immediate purpose is to lead you to place in juxta-position, that very unusual activity of which I have just spoken, with that very peculiar shrill (or harsh) and unequal voice, about whose nationality no two persons could be found to agree, and in whose utterance no syllabification could be detected."

At these words a vague and half-formed conception of the meaning of Dupin flitted over my mind. I seemed to be upon the verge of comprehension, without power to comprehend --as men, at times, find themselves upon the brink of remembrance, without being able, in the end, to remember. My friend went on with his discourse.

"You will see," he said, "that I have shifted the question from the mode of egress to that of ingress. It was my design to convey the idea that both were effected in the same manner, at the same point. Let us now revert to the interior of the room. Let us survey the appearances here. The drawers of the bureau, it is said, had been rifled, although many articles of apparel still remained within them. The conclusion here is absurd. It is a mere guess --a very silly one --and no more. How are we to know that the articles found in the drawers were not all these drawers had originally contained? Madame L'Espanaye and her daughter lived

an exceedingly retired life --saw no company --
seldom went out --had little use for numerous
changes of habiliment. Those found were at least of as
good quality as any likely to be possessed by these
ladies. If a thief had taken any, why did he not take the
best --why did he not take all? In a word, why did he
abandon four thousand francs in gold to encumber
himself with a bundle of linen? The gold was
abandoned. Nearly the whole sum mentioned by
Monsieur Mignaud, the banker, was discovered, in
bags, upon the floor. I wish you, therefore, to discard
from your thoughts the blundering idea of motive,
engendered in the brains of the police by that portion
of the evidence which speaks of money delivered at the
door of the house. Coincidences ten times as
remarkable as this (the delivery of the money, and
murder committed within three days upon the party
receiving it), happen to all of us every hour of our
lives, without attracting even momentary notice.
Coincidences, in general, are great stumbling-blocks
in the way of that class of thinkers who have been
educated to know nothing of the theory of probabilities
-- that theory to which the most glorious objects of
human research are indebted for the most glorious of
illustration. In the present instance, had the gold been
gone, the fact of its delivery three days before would
have formed something more than a coincidence. It
would have been corroborative of this idea of motive.
But, under the real circumstances of the case, if we are
to suppose gold the motive of this outrage, we must
also imagine the perpetrator so vacillating an idiot as
to have abandoned his gold and his motive together.

"Keeping now steadily in mind the points to which I
have drawn your attention --that peculiar voice, that
unusual agility, and that startling absence of motive in

a murder so singularly atrocious as this --let us glance at the butchery itself. Here is a woman strangled to death by manual strength, and thrust up a chimney, head downward. Ordinary assassins employ no such modes of murder as this. Least of all, do they thus dispose of the murdered. In the manner of thrusting the corpse up the chimney, you will admit that there was something excessively outré --something altogether irreconcilable with our common notions of human action, even when we suppose the actors the most depraved of men. Think, too, how great must have been that strength which could have thrust the body up such an aperture so forcibly that the united vigor of several persons was found barely sufficient to drag it down!

"Turn, now, to other indications of the employment of a vigor most marvellous. On the hearth were thick tresses --very thick tresses --of grey human hair. These had been torn out by the roots. You are aware of the great force necessary in tearing thus from the head even twenty or thirty hairs together. You saw the locks in question as well as myself. Their roots (a hideous sight!) were clotted with fragments of the flesh of the scalp --sure token of the prodigious power which had been exerted in uprooting perhaps half a million of hairs at a time. The throat of the old lady was not merely cut, but the head absolutely severed from the body: the instrument was a mere razor. I wish you also to look at the brutal ferocity of these deeds. Of the bruises upon the body of Madame L'Espanaye I do not speak. Monsieur Dumas, and his worthy coadjutor Monsieur Etienne, have pronounced that they were inflicted by some obtuse instrument; and so far these gentlemen are very correct. The obtuse instrument was clearly the stone pavement in the yard, upon which the victim had fallen from the window which looked in upon the bed. This idea, however simple it may now seem, escaped the police for the same reason that the breadth of the shutters escaped them --because, by the affair of the nails, their perceptions had been hermetically sealed against the possibility of the windows having ever been opened at all.

"If now, in addition to all these things, you have properly reflected upon the odd disorder of the chamber, we have gone so far as to combine the ideas of an agility astounding, a strength superhuman, a ferocity brutal, a butchery without motive, a grotesquerie in horror absolutely alien from humanity, and a voice foreign in tone to the ears of men of many nations, and devoid of all distinct or intelligible syllabification. What result, then, has ensued? What impression have I made upon your fancy?"

I felt a creeping of the flesh as Dupin asked me the question. "A madman," I said, "has done this deed --some raving maniac, escaped from a neighboring Maison de Santé."

"In some respects," he replied, "your idea is not irrelevant. But the voices of madmen, even in their wildest paroxysms, are never found to tally with that peculiar voice heard upon the stairs. Madmen are of some nation, and their language, however incoherent in its words, has always the coherence of syllabification. Besides, the hair of a madman is not such as I now hold in my hand. I disentangled this little tuft from the rigidly clutched fingers of Madame L'Espanaye. Tell me what you can make of it."

"Dupin!" I said, completely unnerved; "this hair is most unusual --this is no human hair."

"I have not asserted that it is," said he; "but, before we decide this point, I wish you to glance at the little sketch I have here traced upon this paper. It is a fac-simile drawing of what has been described in one portion of the testimony as 'dark bruises, and deep indentations of finger nails,' upon the throat of Mademoiselle L'Espanaye, and in another, (by Messrs. Dumas and Etienne,) as a 'series of livid spots, evidently the impression of fingers.'

"You will perceive," continued my friend, spreading out the paper upon the table before us, "that this drawing gives the idea of a firm and fixed hold. There is no slipping apparent. Each finger has retained -- possibly until the death of the victim --the fearful grasp by which it originally imbedded itself. Attempt, now, to place all your fingers, at the same time, in the respective impressions as you see them."

I made the attempt in vain.

"We are possibly not giving this matter a fair trial," he said. "The paper is spread out upon a plane surface; but the human throat is cylindrical. Here is a billet of wood, the circumference of which is about that of the throat. Wrap the drawing around it, and try the experiment again."

I did so; but the difficulty was even more obvious than before. "This," I said, "is the mark of no human hand."

"Read now," replied Dupin, "this passage from Cuvier."

It was a minute anatomical and generally descriptive account of the large fulvous Ourang-Outang of the East Indian Islands. The gigantic stature, the prodigious strength and activity, the wild ferocity, and the imitative propensities of these mammalia are sufficiently well known to all. I understood the full horrors of the murder at once.

"The description of the digits," said I, as I made an
end of reading, "is in exact accordance with this
drawing. I see that no animal but an Ourang-Outang,
of the species here mentioned, could have impressed
the indentations as you have traced them. This tuft of
tawny hair, too, is identical in character with that of
the beast of Cuvier. But I cannot possibly comprehend
the particulars of this frightful mystery. Besides, there
were two voices heard in contention, and one of them
was unquestionably the voice of a Frenchman."

"True; and you will remember an expression
attributed almost unanimously, by the evidence, to
this voice, --the expression, 'mon Dieu!' This, under
the circumstances, has been justly characterized by
one of the witnesses (Montani, the confectioner,) as an
expression of remonstrance or expostulation. Upon
these two words, therefore, I have mainly built my
hopes of a full solution of the riddle. A Frenchman was
cognizant of the murder. It is possible --indeed it is
far more than probable --that he was innocent of all
participation in the bloody transactions which took
place. The Ourang-Outang may have escaped from
him. He may have traced it to the chamber; but, under
the agitating circumstances which ensued, he could
never have re-captured it. It is still at large. I will not
pursue these guesses --for I have no right to call them
more --since the shades of reflection upon which they
are based are scarcely of sufficient depth to be
appreciable by my own intellect, and since I could not
pretend to make them intelligible to the understanding
of another. We will call them guesses then, and speak
of them as such. If the Frenchman in question is
indeed, as I suppose, innocent of this atrocity, this
advertisement, which I left last night, upon our return
home, at the office of 'Le Monde,' (a paper devoted to

the shipping interest, and much sought by sailors,)
will bring him to our residence."

He handed me a paper, and I read thus:

CAUGHT -- In the Bois de Boulogne, early in the
morning of the ____ inst., (the morning of the
murder,) a very large, tawny Ourang-Outang of the
Bornese species. The owner, (who is ascertained to be
a sailor, belonging to a Maltese vessel,) may have the
animal again, upon identifying it satisfactorily, and
paying a few charges arising from its capture and
keeping. Call at No. ____ , Rue ____, Faubourg St.
Germain --au troisiême.

"How was it possible," I asked, "that you should
know the man to be a sailor, and belonging to a
Maltese vessel?"

"I do not know it," said Dupin. "I am not sure of it.
Here, however, is a small piece of ribbon, which from
its form, and from its greasy appearance, has evidently
been used in tying the hair in one of those long queues
of which sailors are so fond. Moreover, this knot is one
which few besides sailors can tie, and is peculiar to the
Maltese. I picked the ribbon up at the foot of the
lightning-rod. It could not have belonged to either of
the deceased. Now if, after all, I am wrong in my
induction from this ribbon, that the Frenchman was a
sailor belonging to a Maltese vessel, still I can have
done no harm in saying what I did in the
advertisement. If I am in error, he will merely suppose
that I have been misled by some circumstance into
which he will not take the trouble to inquire. But if I
am right, a great point is gained. Cognizant although
innocent of the murder, the Frenchman will naturally
hesitate about replying to the advertisement --about
demanding the Ourang-Outang. He will reason thus: -
-'I am innocent; I am poor; my Ourang-Outang is of

great value --to one in my circumstances a fortune of itself --why should I lose it through idle apprehensions of danger? Here it is, within my grasp. It was found in the Bois de Boulogne --at a vast distance from the scene of that butchery. How can it ever be suspected that a brute beast should have done the deed? The police are at fault --they have failed to procure the slightest clew. Should they even trace the animal, it would be impossible to prove me cognizant of the murder, or to implicate me in guilt on account of that cognizance. Above all, I am known. The advertiser designates me as the possessor of the beast. I am not sure to what limit his knowledge may extend. Should I avoid claiming a property of so great value, which it is known that I possess, I will render the animal at least, liable to suspicion. It is not my policy to attract attention either to myself or to the beast. I will answer the advertisement, get the Ourang-Outang, and keep it close until this matter has blown over.' "

At this moment we heard a step upon the stairs.

"Be ready," said Dupin, "with your pistols, but neither use them nor show them until at a signal from myself."

The front door of the house had been left open, and the visiter had entered, without ringing, and advanced several steps upon the staircase. Now, however, he seemed to hesitate. Presently we heard him descending. Dupin was moving quickly to the door, when we again heard him coming up. He did not turn back a second time, but stepped up with decision, and rapped at the door of our chamber.

"Come in," said Dupin, in a cheerful and hearty tone.

A man entered. He was a sailor, evidently, --a tall, stout, and muscular-looking person, with a certain

dare-devil expression of countenance, not altogether
unprepossessing. His face, greatly sunburnt, was more
than half hidden by whisker and mustachio. He had
with him a huge oaken cudgel, but appeared to be
otherwise unarmed. He bowed awkwardly, and bade us
"good evening," in French accents, which, although
somewhat Neufchatelish, were still sufficiently
indicative of a Parisian origin.

"Sit down, my friend," said Dupin. "I suppose you
have called about the Ourang-Outang. Upon my word,
I almost envy you the possession of him; a remarkably
fine, and no doubt a very valuable animal. How old do
you suppose him to be?"

The sailor drew a long breath, with the air of a man
relieved of some intolerable burden, and then replied,
in an assured tone:

"I have no way of telling --but he can't be more
than four or five years old. Have you got him here?"

"Oh no; we had no conveniences for keeping him
here. He is at a livery stable in the Rue Dubourg, just
by. You can get him in the morning. Of course you are
prepared to identify the property?"

"To be sure I am, sir."

"I shall be sorry to part with him," said Dupin.

"I don't mean that you should be at all this trouble
for nothing, sir," said the man. "Couldn't expect it. Am
very willing to pay a reward for the finding of the
animal -- that is to say, any thing in reason."

"Well," replied my friend, "that is all very fair, to be
sure. Let me think! --what should I have? Oh! I will
tell you. My reward shall be this. You shall give me all
the information in your power about these murders in
the Rue Morgue."

Dupin said the last words in a very low tone, and
very quietly. Just as quietly, too, he walked toward the

door, locked it, and put the key in his pocket. He then
drew a pistol from his bosom and placed it, without
the least flurry, upon the table.

The sailor's face flushed up as if he were struggling
with suffocation. He started to his feet and grasped his
cudgel; but the next moment he fell back into his seat,
trembling violently, and with the countenance of death
itself. He spoke not a word. I pitied him from the
bottom of my heart.

"My friend," said Dupin, in a kind tone, "you are
alarming yourself unnecessarily --you are indeed. We
mean you no harm whatever. I pledge you the honor of
a gentleman, and of a Frenchman, that we intend you
no injury. I perfectly well know that you are innocent
of the atrocities in the Rue Morgue. It will not do,
however, to deny that you are in some measure
implicated in them. From what I have already said, you
must know that I have had means of information
about this matter --means of which you could never
have dreamed. Now the thing stands thus. You have
done nothing which you could have avoided --
nothing, certainly, which renders you culpable. You
were not even guilty of robbery, when you might have
robbed with impunity. You have nothing to conceal.
You have no reason for concealment. On the other
hand, you are bound by every principle of honor to
confess all you know. An innocent man is now
imprisoned, charged with that crime of which you can
point out the perpetrator."

The sailor had recovered his presence of mind, in a
great measure, while Dupin uttered these words; but
his original boldness of bearing was all gone.

"So help me God," said he, after a brief pause, "I will
tell you all I know about this affair; --but I do not
expect you to believe one half I say --I would be a fool

indeed if I did. Still, I am innocent, and I will make a clean breast if I die for it."

What he stated was, in substance, this. He had lately made a voyage to the Indian Archipelago. A party, of which he formed one, landed at Borneo, and passed into the interior on an excursion of pleasure. Himself and a companion had captured the Ourang- Outang. This companion dying, the animal fell into his own exclusive possession. After great trouble, occasioned by the intractable ferocity of his captive during the home voyage, he at length succeeded in lodging it safely at his own residence in Paris, where, not to attract toward himself the unpleasant curiosity of his neighbors, he kept it carefully secluded, until such time as it should recover from a wound in the foot, received from a splinter on board ship. His ultimate design was to sell it.

Returning home from some sailors' frolic the night, or rather in the morning of the murder, he found the beast occupying his own bed-room, into which it had broken from a closet adjoining, where it had been, as was thought, securely confined. Razor in hand, and fully lathered, it was sitting before a looking-glass, attempting the operation of shaving, in which it had no doubt previously watched its master through the key-hole of the closet. Terrified at the sight of so dangerous a weapon in the possession of an animal so ferocious, and so well able to use it, the man, for some moments, was at a loss what to do. He had been accustomed, however, to quiet the creature, even in its fiercest moods, by the use of a whip, and to this he now resorted. Upon sight of it, the Ourang-Outang sprang at once through the door of the chamber, down the stairs, and thence, through a window, unfortunately open, into the street.

The Frenchman followed in despair; the ape, razor still in hand, occasionally stopping to look back and gesticulate at its pursuer, until the latter had nearly come up with it. It then again made off. In this manner the chase continued for a long time. The streets were profoundly quiet, as it was nearly three o'clock in the morning. In passing down an alley in the rear of the Rue Morgue, the fugitive's attention was arrested by a light gleaming from the open window of Madame L'Espanaye's chamber, in the fourth story of her house. Rushing to the building, it perceived the lightning-rod, clambered up with inconceivable agility, grasped the shutter, which was thrown fully back against the wall, and, by its means, swung itself directly upon the headboard of the bed. The whole feat did not occupy a minute. The shutter was kicked open again by the Ourang-Outang as it entered the room.

The sailor, in the meantime, was both rejoiced and perplexed. He had strong hopes of now recapturing the brute, as it could scarcely escape from the trap into which it had ventured, except by the rod, where it might be intercepted as it came down. On the other hand, there was much cause for anxiety as to what it might do in the house. This latter reflection urged the man still to follow the fugitive. A lightning-rod is ascended without difficulty, especially by a sailor; but, when he had arrived as high as the window, which lay far to his left, his career was stopped; the most that he could accomplish was to reach over so as to obtain a glimpse of the interior of the room. At this glimpse he nearly fell from his hold through excess of horror. Now it was that those hideous shrieks arose upon the night, which had startled from slumber the inmates of the Rue Morgue. Madame L'Espanaye and her daughter, habited in their night clothes, had apparently been occupied in arranging some papers in the iron chest already mentioned, which had been wheeled into the middle of the room. It was open, and its contents lay beside it on the floor. The victims must have been sitting with their backs toward the window; and, from the time elapsing between the ingress of the beast and the screams, it seems probable that it was not immediately perceived. The flapping-to of the shutter would naturally have been attributed to the wind.

As the sailor looked in, the gigantic animal had seized Madame L'Espanaye by the hair, (which was loose, as she had been combing it,) and was flourishing the razor about her face, in imitation of the motions of a barber. The daughter lay prostrate and motionless; she had swooned. The screams and struggles of the old lady (during which the hair was torn from her head) had the effect of changing the probably pacific purposes of the Ourang-Outang into those of wrath. With one determined sweep of its muscular arm it nearly severed her head from her body. The sight of blood inflamed its anger into phrenzy. Gnashing its teeth, and flashing fire from its eyes, it flew upon the body of the girl, and imbedded its fearful talons in her throat, retaining its grasp until she expired. Its wandering and wild glances fell at this moment upon the head of the bed, over which the face of its master, rigid with horror, was just discernible. The fury of the beast, who no doubt bore still in mind the dreaded whip, was instantly converted into fear. Conscious of having deserved punishment, it seemed desirous of concealing its bloody deeds, and skipped about the chamber in an agony of nervous agitation; throwing down and breaking the furniture as it moved, and dragging the bed from the bedstead. In conclusion, it seized first the corpse of the daughter, and thrust it

up the chimney, as it was found; then that of the old
lady, which it immediately hurled through the window
headlong.

As the ape approached the casement with its
mutilated burden, the sailor shrank aghast to the rod,
and, rather gliding than clambering down it, hurried at
once home --dreading the consequences of the
butchery, and gladly abandoning, in his terror, all
solicitude about the fate of the Ourang-Outang. The
words heard by the party upon the staircase were the
Frenchman's exclamations of horror and affright,
commingled with the fiendish jabberings of the brute.

I have scarcely anything to add. The Ourang-Outang
must have escaped from the chamber, by the rod, just
before the breaking of the door. It must have closed
the window as it passed through it. It was
subsequently caught by the owner himself, who
obtained for it a very large sum at the Jardin des
Plantes. Le Bon was instantly released, upon our
narration of the circumstances (with some comments
from Dupin) at the bureau of the Prefect of Police. This
functionary, however well disposed to my friend, could
not altogether conceal his chagrin at the turn which
affairs had taken, and was fain to indulge in a sarcasm
or two, about the propriety of every person minding
his own business.

"Let him talk," said Dupin, who had not thought it
necessary to reply. "Let him discourse; it will ease his
conscience. I am satisfied with having defeated him in
his own castle. Nevertheless, that he failed in the
solution of this mystery, is by no means that matter
for wonder which he supposes it; for, in truth, our
friend the Prefect is somewhat too cunning to be
profound. In his wisdom is no stamen. It is all head
and no body, like the pictures of the Goddess Laverna,

-- or, at best, all head and shoulders, like a codfish. But he is a good creature after all. I like him especially for one master stroke of cant, by which he has attained his reputation for ingenuity. I mean the way he has 'de nier ce qui est, et d'expliquer ce qui n'est pas.' "*

The Fall of the House of Usher

It was a dark and soundless day near the end of the year, and clouds were hanging low in the heavens. All day I had been riding on horseback through country with little life or beauty; and in the early evening I came within view of the House of Usher. I do not know how it was — but, with my first sight of the building, a sense of heavy sadness filled my spirit. I looked at the scene before me — at the house itself — at the ground around it — at the cold stone walls of the building — at its empty eye-like windows — and at a few dead trees — I looked at this scene, I say, with a complete sadness of soul which was no healthy, earthly feeling. There was a coldness, a sickening of the heart, in which I could discover nothing to lighten the weight I felt. What was it, I asked myself, what was it that was so fearful, so frightening in my view of the House of Usher? This was a question to which I could find no answer. I stopped my horse beside the building, on the edge of a dark and quiet lake. There, I could see reflected in the water a clear picture of the dead trees, and of the house and its empty eye-like windows. 23 Edgar Allan Poe: Storyteller I was now going to spend several weeks in this house of sadness — this house of gloom. Its owner was named Roderick Usher. We had been friends when we were boys; but many years had passed since our last meeting. A letter from him had reached me, a wild letter which demanded that I reply by coming to see him. He wrote of an illness of the body — of a sickness of the mind — and of a desire to see me — his best and indeed his only friend. It was the manner in which all this was said — it was the heart in it — which did not allow me to say no. Although as boys we had been together, I really knew little about my friend. I knew, however, that his family, a very old one, had long been famous for its understanding of all the arts and for many quiet acts of kindness to the poor. I had learned too that the family had never been a large one, with many branches. The name had passed always from father to son, and when people spoke of the "House of Usher,"

they included both the family and the family home. I
again looked up from the picture of the house reflected
in the lake to the house itself. A strange idea grew in
my mind — an idea so strange that I tell it only to
show the force of the feelings which laid their weight
on me. I really believed that around the whole house,
and the ground around it, the air itself was different. It
was not the air of heaven. It rose from the dead,
decaying trees, from the gray walls, and the quiet lake.
It was a sickly, unhealthy air that I could see, slow-
moving, heavy, and gray. Shaking off from my spirit
what must have been a dream, I looked more carefully
at the building itself. The most noticeable thing about
it seemed to be its great age. None of the walls had
fallen, yet the stones appeared to be in a condition of
advanced decay. Perhaps the careful eye would have
discovered the beginning of a break in the front of the
building, a crack making its way from the top down
the wall until it became lost in the dark waters of the
lake. I rode over a short bridge to the house. A man
who worked in the house — a servant — took my
horse, and I entered. Another servant, of quiet step, led
me without a word through many dark turnings to the
room of his master. Much that I met on the way added,
I do not know how, to the strangeness of which I have
already spoken. While the objects around me — the
dark wall coverings, the blackness of the floors, and
the things brought home from long forgotten wars —
24 Edgar Allan Poe while these things were like the
things I had known since I was a baby — while I
admitted that all this was only what I had expected —
I was still surprised at the strange ideas which grew in
my mind from these simple things. The room I came
into was very large and high. The windows were high,
and pointed at the top, and so far above the black floor

that they were quite out of reach. Only a little light, red
in color, made its way through the glass, and served to
lighten the nearer and larger objects. My eyes,
however, tried and failed to see into the far, high
corners of the room. Dark coverings hung upon the
walls. The many chairs and tables had been used for a
long, long time. Books lay around the room, but could
give it no sense of life. I felt sadness hanging over
everything. No escape from this deep cold gloom
seemed possible. As I entered the room, Usher stood
up from where he had been lying and met me with a
warmth which at first I could not believe was real. A
look, however, at his face told me that every word he
spoke was true. We sat down; and for some moments,
while he said nothing, I looked at him with a feeling of
sad surprise. Surely, no man had ever before changed
as Roderick Usher had! Could this be the friend of my
early years? It is true that his face had always been
unusual. He had gray-white skin; eyes large and full of
light; lips not bright in color, but of a beautiful shape;
a well-shaped nose; hair of great softness — a face
that was not easy to forget. And now the increase in
this strangeness of his face had caused so great a
change that I almost did not know him. The horrible
white of his skin, and the strange light in his eyes,
surprised me and even made me afraid. His hair had
been allowed to grow, and in its softness it did not fall
around his face but seemed to lie upon the air. I could
not, even with an effort, see in my friend the
appearance of a simple human being. In his manner, I
saw at once, changes came and went; and I soon found
that this resulted from his attempt to quiet a very
great nervousness. I had indeed been prepared for
something like this, partly by his letter and partly by
remembering him as a boy. His actions were first too

quick and then too quiet. Sometimes his voice, slow and trembling with fear, quickly changed to a strong, heavy, carefully spaced, too perfectly controlled manner. It was in this manner that he 25 Edgar Allan Poe: Storyteller spoke of the purpose of my visit, of his desire to see me, and of the deep delight and strength he expected me to give him. He told me what he believed to be the nature of his illness. It was, he said, a family sickness, and one from which he could not hope to grow better — but it was, he added at once, only a nervous illness which would without doubt soon pass away. It showed itself in a number of strange feelings. Some of these, as he told me of them, interested me but were beyond my understanding; perhaps the way in which he told me of them added to their strangeness. He suffered much from a sickly increase in the feeling of all the senses; he could eat only the most tasteless food; all flowers smelled too strongly for his nose; his eyes were hurt by even a little light; and there were few sounds which did not fill him with horror. A certain kind of sick fear was completely his master. "I shall die," he said. "I shall die! I must die of this fool's sickness. In this way, this way and no other way, I shall be lost. I fear what will happen in the future, not for what happens, but for the result of what happens. I have, indeed, no fear of pain, but only fear of its result — of terror! I feel that the time will soon arrive when I must lose my life, and my mind, and my soul, together, in some last battle with that horrible enemy: fear!" 26 p Edgar Allan Poe The Fall of the House of Usher Part Two Roderick Usher, whom I had known as a boy, was now ill and had asked me to come to help him. When I arrived I felt something strange and fearful about the great old stone house, about the lake in front of it, and about

Usher himself. He appeared not like a human being, but like a spirit that had come back from beyond the grave. It was an illness, he said, from which he would surely die. He called his sickness fear. "I have," he said, "no fear of pain, but only the fear of its result — of terror. I feel that the time will soon arrive when I must lose my life, and my mind, and my soul, together, in some last battle with that horrible enemy: fear!" I learned also, but slowly, and through broken words with doubtful meaning, another strange fact about the condition of Usher's mind. He had certain sick fears about the house in which he lived, and he had not stepped out of it for many years. He felt that the house, with its gray walls and the quiet lake around it, had somehow through the long years gotten a strong hold on his spirit. 27 Edgar Allan Poe: Storyteller He said, however, that much of the gloom which lay so heavily on him was probably caused by something more plainly to be seen — by the long-continued illness — indeed, the coming death — of a dearly loved sister — his only company for many years. Except for himself, she was the last member of his family on earth. "When she dies," he said, with a sadness which I can never forget, "when she dies, I will be the last of the old, old family — the House of Usher." While he spoke, the lady Madeline (for so she was called) passed slowly through a distant part of the room, and without seeing that I was there, went on. I looked at her with a complete and wondering surprise and with some fear — and yet I found I could not explain to myself such feelings. My eyes followed her. When she came to a door and it closed behind her, my eyes turned to the face of her brother — but he had put his face in his hands, and I could see only that the thin fingers through which his tears were flowing were

whiter than ever before. The illness of the lady
Madeline had long been beyond the help of her
doctors. She seemed to care about nothing. Slowly her
body had grown thin and weak, and often for a short
period she would fall into a sleep like the sleep of the
dead. So far she had not been forced to stay in bed; but
by the evening of the day I arrived at the house, the
power of her destroyer (as her brother told me that
night) was too strong for her. I learned that my one
sight of her would probably be the last I would have —
that the lady, at least while living, would be seen by
me no more. For several days following, her name was
not spoken by either Usher or myself; and during this
period I was busy with efforts to lift my friend out of
his sadness and gloom. We painted and read together;
or listened, as if in a dream, to the wild music he
played. And so, as a warmer and more loving
friendship grew between us, I saw more clearly the
uselessness of all attempts to bring happiness to a
mind from which only darkness came, spreading upon
all objects in the world its never-ending gloom. I shall
always remember the hours I spent with the master of
the House of Usher. Yet I would fail in any attempt to
give an idea of the true character of the things we did
together. There was a strange light over everything.
The paintings which he made made me tremble, 28
Edgar Allan Poe though I know not why. To tell of
them is beyond the power of written words. If ever a
man painted an idea, that man was Roderick Usher.
For me at least there came out of his pictures a sense
of fear and wonder. One of these pictures may be told,
although weakly, in words. It showed the inside of a
room where the dead might be placed, with low walls,
white and plain. It seemed to be very deep under the
earth. There was no door, no window; and no light or

fire burned; yet a river of light flowed through it, filling it with a horrible, ghastly brightness. I have spoken of that sickly condition of the senses, which made most music painful for Usher to hear. The notes he could listen to with pleasure were very few. It was this fact, perhaps, that made the music he played so different from most music. But the wild beauty of his playing could not be explained. The words of one of his songs, called "The Haunted Palace," I have easily remembered. In it I thought I saw, and for the first time, that Usher knew very well that his mind was weakening. This song told of a great house where a king lived — a palace — in a green valley, where all was light and color and beauty, and the air was sweet. In the palace were two bright windows through which people in that happy valley could hear music and could see smiling ghosts — spirits — moving around the king. The palace door was of the richest materials, in red and white; through it came other spirits whose only duty was to sing in their beautiful voices about how wise their king was. But a dark change came, the song continued, and now those who enter the valley see through the windows, in a red light, shapes that move to broken music; while through the door, now colorless, a ghastly river of ghosts, laughing but no longer smiling, rushes out forever. Our talk of this song led to another strange idea in Usher's mind. He believed that plants could feel and think, and not only plants, but rocks and water as well. He believed that the gray stones of his house, and the small plants growing on the stones, and the decaying trees, had a power over him that made him what he was. Our books — the books which, for years, had fed the sick man's mind — were, as might be supposed, of this same wild character. Some of these books Usher sat and studied for hours. His chief delight was found in reading one very old book, written for some forgotten church, telling of the Watch over the Dead. 29 Edgar Allan Poe: Storyteller At last, one evening he told me that the lady Madeline was alive no more. He said he was going to keep her body for a time in one of the many vaults inside the walls of the building. The worldly reason he gave for this was one with which I felt I had to agree. He had decided to do this because of the nature of her illness, because of the strange interest and questions of her doctors, and because of the great distance to the graveyard where members of his family were placed in the earth. We two carried her body to its resting place. The vault in which we placed it was small and dark, and in ages past it must have seen strange and bloody scenes. It lay deep below that part of the building where I myself slept. The thick door was of iron, and because of its great weight made a loud, hard sound when it was opened and closed. As we placed the lady Madeline in this room of horror I saw for the first time the great likeness between brother and sister, and Usher told me then that they were twins — they had been born on the same day. For that reason the understanding between them had always been great, and the tie that held them together very strong. We looked down at the dead face one last time, and I was filled with wonder. As she lay there, the lady Madeline looked not dead but asleep — still soft and warm — though to the touch cold as the stones around us. 30 p Edgar Allan Poe The Fall of the House of Usher Part Three I was visiting an old friend of mine, Roderick Usher, in his old stone house, his palace, where a feeling of death hung on the air. I saw how fear was pressing on his heart and mind. Now his only sister, the lady Madeline, had died and we had put her body

in its resting place, in a room inside the cold walls of
the palace, a damp, dark vault, a fearful place. As we
looked down upon her face, I saw that there was a
strong likeness between the two. "Indeed," said Usher,
"we were born on the same day, and the tie between
us has always been strong." We did not long look
down at her, for fear and wonder filled our hearts.
There was still a little color in her face and there
seemed to be a smile on her lips. We closed the heavy
iron door and returned to the rooms above, which were
hardly less gloomy than the vault. And now a change
came in the sickness of my friend's mind. He went
from room to room with a hurried step. His face was, if
possible, whiter and more ghastly than before, and the
light in his eyes had 31 Edgar Allan Poe: Storyteller
gone. The trembling in his voice seemed to show the
greatest fear. At times he sat looking at nothing for
hours, as if listening to some sound I could not hear. I
felt his condition, slowly but certainly, gaining power
over me; I felt that his wild ideas were becoming fixed
in my own mind. As I was going to bed late in the
night of the seventh or eighth day after we placed the
lady Madeline within the vault, I experienced the full
power of such feelings. Sleep did not come — while
the hours passed. My mind fought against the
nervousness. I tried to believe that much, if not all, of
what I felt was due to the gloomy room, to the dark
wall coverings, which in a rising wind moved on the
walls. But my efforts were useless. A trembling I could
not stop filled my body, and fear without reason
caught my heart. I sat up, looking into the darkness of
my room, listening — I do not know why — to certain
low sounds which came when the storm was quiet. A
feeling of horror lay upon me like a heavy weight. I put
on my clothes and began walking nervously around the

room. I had been walking for a very short time when I heard a light step coming toward my door. I knew it was Usher. In a moment I saw him at my door, as usual very white, but there was a wild laugh in his eyes. Even so, I was glad to have his company. "And have you not seen it?" he said. He hurried to one of the windows and opened it to the storm. The force of the entering wind nearly lifted us from our feet. It was, indeed, a stormy but beautiful night, and wildly strange. The heavy, low-hanging clouds which seemed to press down upon the house, flew from all directions against each other, always returning and never passing away in the distance. With their great thickness they cut off all light from the moon and the stars. But we could see them because they were lighted from below by the air itself, which we could see, rising from the dark lake and from the stones of the house itself. "You must not — you shall not look out at this!" I said to Usher, as I led him from the window to a seat. "This appearance which surprises you so has been seen in other places, too. Perhaps the lake is the cause. Let us close this window; the air is cold. Here is one of the stories you like best. I will read and you shall listen and thus we will live through this fearful night together." 32 Edgar Allan Poe The old book which I had picked up was one written by a fool for fools to read, and it was not, in truth, one that Usher liked. It was, however, the only one within easy reach. He seemed to listen quietly. Then I came to a part of the story in which a man, a strong man full of wine, begins to break down a door, and the sound of the dry wood as it breaks can be heard through all the forest around him. Here I stopped, for it seemed to me that from some very distant part of the house sounds came to my ears like those of which I had been reading. It

must have been this likeness that had made me notice
them, for the sounds themselves, with the storm still
increasing, were nothing to stop or interest me. I
continued the story, and read how the man, now
entering through the broken door, discovers a strange
and terrible animal of the kind so often found in these
old stories. He strikes it and it falls, with such a cry
that he has to close his ears with his hands. Here again
I stopped. There could be no doubt. This time I did
hear a distant sound, very much like the cry of the
animal in the story. I tried to control myself so that my
friend would see nothing of what I felt. I was not
certain that he had heard the sound, although he had
clearly changed in some way. He had slowly moved his
chair so that I could not see him well. I did see that his
lips were moving as if he were speaking to himself. His
head had dropped forward, but I knew he was not
asleep, for his eyes were open and he was moving his
body from side to side. I began reading again, and
quickly came to a part of the story where a heavy piece
of iron falls on a stone floor with a ringing sound.
These words had just passed my lips when I heard
clearly, but from far away, a loud ringing sound — as
if something of iron had indeed fallen heavily upon a
stone floor, or as if an iron door had closed. I lost
control of myself completely, and jumped up from my
chair. Usher still sat, moving a little from side to side.
His eyes were turned to the floor. I rushed to his chair.
As I placed my hand on his shoulder, I felt that his
whole body was trembling; a sickly smile touched his
lips; he spoke in a low, quick, and nervous voice as if
he did not know I was there. 33 Edgar Allan Poe:
Storyteller "Yes!" he said. "I heard it! Many minutes,
many hours, many days have I heard it — but I did not
dare to speak! We have put her living in the vault! Did I

not say that my senses were too strong? I heard her first movements many days ago — yet I did not dare to speak! And now, that story — but the sounds were hers! Oh, where shall I run?! She is coming — coming to ask why I put her there too soon. I hear her footsteps on the stairs. I hear the heavy beating of her heart." Here he jumped up and cried as if he were giving up his soul: "I tell you, she now stands at the door!!" The great door to which he was pointing now slowly opened. It was the work of the rushing wind, perhaps — but no — outside that door a shape did stand, the tall figure, in its grave-clothes, of the lady Madeline of Usher. There was blood upon her white dress, and the signs of her terrible efforts to escape were upon every part of her thin form. For a moment she remained trembling at the door; then, with a low cry, she fell heavily in upon her brother; in her pain, as she died at last, she carried him down with her, down to the floor. He too was dead, killed by his own fear. I rushed from the room; I rushed from the house. I ran. The storm was around me in all its strength as I crossed the bridge. Suddenly a wild light moved along the ground at my feet, and I turned to see where it could have come from, for only the great house and its darkness were behind me. The light was that of the full moon, of a bloodred moon, which was now shining through that break in the front wall, that crack which I thought I had seen when I first saw the palace. Then only a little crack, it now widened as I watched. A strong wind came rushing over me — the whole face of the moon appeared. I saw the great walls falling apart. There was a long and stormy shouting sound — and the deep black lake closed darkly over all that remained of the house of usher.

Tamerlane

Kind solace in a dying hour!
   Such, father, is not (now) my theme—
I will not madly deem that power
   Of Earth may shrive me of the sin
   Unearthly pride hath revell'd in—
I have no time to dote or dream:
You call it hope—that fire of fire!
It is but agony of desire:
If I can hope—Oh God! I can—
   Its fount is holier—more divine—
I would not call thee fool, old man,

But such is not a gift of thine.
Know thou the secret of a spirit
   Bow'd from its wild pride into shame.
O! yearning heart! I did inherit
   Thy withering portion with the fame,
The searing glory which hath shone
Amid the jewels of my throne,
Halo of Hell! and with a pain
Not Hell shall make me fear again—
O! craving heart, for the lost flowers
And sunshine of my summer hours!
Th' undying voice of that dead time,
With its interminable chime,
Rings, in the spirit of a spell,
Upon thy emptiness—a knell.
I have not always been as now:
The fever'd diadem on my brow
   I claim'd and won usurpingly—
Hath not the same fierce heirdom given
   Rome to the Caesar—this to me?
     The heritage of a kingly mind,
And a proud spirit which hath striven
     Triumphantly with human kind.
On mountain soil I first drew life:
   The mists of the Taglay have shed
   Nightly their dews upon my head,
And, I believe, the winged strife
And tumult of the headlong air
Have nestled in my very hair.
So late from Heaven—that dew—it fell
   (Mid dreams of an unholy night)
Upon me—with the touch of Hell,
   While the red flashing of the light
From clouds that hung, like banners, o'er,
   Appeared to my half-closing eye
   The pageantry of monarchy,

And the deep trumpet-thunder's roar
    Came hurriedly upon me, telling
        Of human battle, where my voice,
    My own voice, silly child!—was swelling
        (O! how my spirit would rejoice,
And leap within me at the cry)
The battle-cry of Victory!
The rain came down upon my head
    Unshelter'd—and the heavy wind
    Was giantlike—so thou, my mind!—
It was but man, I thought, who shed
    Laurels upon me: and the rush—
The torrent of the chilly air
Gurgled within my ear the crush
    Of empires—with the captive's prayer—
The hum of suiters—and the tone
Of flattery 'round a sovereign's throne.
My passions, from that hapless hour,
    Usurp'd a tyranny which men
Have deem'd, since I have reach'd to power;
        My innate nature—be it so:
    But, father, there liv'd one who, then,
Then—in my boyhood—when their fire
        Burn'd with a still intenser glow,
(For passion must, with youth, expire)
    E'en then who knew this iron heart
    In woman's weakness had a part.
I have no words—alas!—to tell
The loveliness of loving well!
Nor would I now attempt to trace
The more than beauty of a face
Whose lineaments, upon my mind,
Are—shadows on th' unstable wind:
Thus I remember having dwelt
Some page of early lore upon,
With loitering eye, till I have felt

The letters—with their meaning—melt
To fantasies—with none.
O, she was worthy of all love!
Love—as in infancy was mine—
'Twas such as angel minds above
Might envy; her young heart the shrine
On which my ev'ry hope and thought
    Were incense—then a goodly gift,
        For they were childish—and upright—
Pure—as her young example taught:
    Why did I leave it, and, adrift,
        Trust to the fire within, for light?
We grew in age—and love—together,
    Roaming the forest, and the wild;
My breast her shield in wintry weather—
    And, when the friendly sunshine smil'd,
And she would mark the opening skies,
I saw no Heaven—but in her eyes.
Young Love's first lesson is—the heart:
    For 'mid that sunshine, and those smiles,
When, from our little cares apart,
    And laughing at her girlish wiles,
I'd throw me on her throbbing breast,
    And pour my spirit out in tears—
There was no need to speak the rest—
    No need to quiet any fears
Of her—who ask'd no reason why,
But turn'd on me her quiet eye!
Yet more than worthy of the love
My spirit struggled with, and strove,
When, on the mountain peak, alone,
Ambition lent it a new tone—
I had no being—but in thee:
    The world, and all it did contain
In the earth—the air—the sea—
    Its joy—its little lot of pain

That was new pleasure—the ideal,
    Dim, vanities of dreams by night—
And dimmer nothings which were real—
    (Shadows—and a more shadowy light!)
Parted upon their misty wings,
        And, so, confusedly, became
        Thine image, and—a name—a name!
Two separate—yet most intimate things.
I was ambitious—have you known
        The passion, father? You have not:
A cottager, I mark'd a throne
Of half the world as all my own,
        And murmur'd at such lowly lot—
But, just like any other dream,
        Upon the vapour of the dew
My own had past, did not the beam
        Of beauty which did while it thro'
The minute—the hour—the day—oppress
My mind with double loveliness.
We walk'd together on the crown
Of a high mountain which look'd down
Afar from its proud natural towers
    Of rock and forest, on the hills—
The dwindled hills! begirt with bowers
    And shouting with a thousand rills.
I spoke to her of power and pride,
    But mystically—in such guise
That she might deem it nought beside
    The moment's converse; in her eyes
I read, perhaps too carelessly—
    A mingled feeling with my own—
The flush on her bright cheek, to me
    Seem'd to become a queenly throne
Too well that I should let it be
    Light in the wilderness alone.
I wrapp'd myself in grandeur then,

And donn'd a visionary crown—
    Yet it was not that Fantasy
    Had thrown her mantle over me—
But that, among the rabble—men,
    Lion ambition is chain'd down—
And crouches to a keeper's hand—
Not so in deserts where the grand
The wild—the terrible conspire
With their own breath to fan his fire.
Look 'round thee now on Samarcand!—
    Is not she queen of Earth? her pride
Above all cities? in her hand
    Their destinies? in all beside
Of glory which the world hath known
Stands she not nobly and alone?
Falling—her veriest stepping-stone
Shall form the pedestal of a throne—
And who her sovereign? Timour—he
    Whom the astonished people saw
Striding o'er empires haughtily
    A diadem'd outlaw—
O! human love! thou spirit given,
On Earth, of all we hope in Heaven!
Which fall'st into the soul like rain
Upon the Siroc wither'd plain,
And failing in thy power to bless
But leav'st the heart a wilderness!
Idea! which bindest life around
With music of so strange a sound
And beauty of so wild a birth—
Farewell! for I have won the Earth!
When Hope, the eagle that tower'd, could see
    No cliff beyond him in the sky,
His pinions were bent droopingly—
    And homeward turn'd his soften'd eye.
'Twas sunset: when the sun will part

There comes a sullenness of heart
To him who still would look upon
The glory of the summer sun.
That soul will hate the ev'ning mist,
So often lovely, and will list
To the sound of the coming darkness (known
To those whose spirits hearken) as one
Who, in a dream of night, would fly
But cannot from a danger nigh.
What tho' the moon—the white moon
Shed all the splendour of her noon,
Her smile is chilly—and her beam,
In that time of dreariness, will seem
(So like you gather in your breath)
A portrait taken after death.
And boyhood is a summer sun
Whose waning is the dreariest one—
For all we live to know is known,
And all we seek to keep hath flown—
Let life, then, as the day-flower, fall
With the noon-day beauty—which is all.
I reach'd my home—my home no more—
    For all had flown who made it so—
I pass'd from out its mossy door,
    And, tho' my tread was soft and low,
A voice came from the threshold stone
Of one whom I had earlier known—
    O! I defy thee, Hell, to show
    On beds of fire that burn below,
    A humbler heart—a deeper wo—
Father, I firmly do believe—
    I know—for Death, who comes for me
        From regions of the blest afar,
Where there is nothing to deceive,
        Hath left his iron gate ajar,
    And rays of truth you cannot see

Are flashing thro' Eternity—
I do believe that Eblis hath
A snare in ev'ry human path—
Else how, when in the holy grove
I wandered of the idol, Love,
Who daily scents his snowy wings
With incense of burnt offerings
From the most unpolluted things,
Whose pleasant bowers are yet so riven
Above with trelliced rays from Heaven
No mote may shun—no tiniest fly
The light'ning of his eagle eye—
How was it that Ambition crept,
    Unseen, amid the revels there,
Till growing bold, he laughed and leapt
    In the tangles of Love's very hair?

Editor's Note– Much of Poe's poetic works reflect themes of love, loss, and regret. However, his short stories veered more toward themes of murder, torture, and even insanity. His work was not always welcome or positively received because often it was simply too scary or sad. In spite of his often depressing tone, his poetry and short stories have left an indelible mark on literature, influencing future writers and even cinema.
 I hope you enjoyed this selection.
Valery J. Elias